Flashbacks and Premonitions

T0151452

Also by Jon Longhi

Bricks and Anchors

The Rise and Fall of Third Leg

Wake Up and Smell the Beer

FLaSHbacKS and PreMONitiONS

Stories

by

JON LONGHi

MaNic D PreSS
SaN FranciSco

For Phoebe

Cover illustration by R. Crumb
Cover design by Scott Idleman/Blink

ISBN 978-0-916397-54-8
Printed in Canada

Library of Congress Cataloging-in-Publication Data

Longhi, Jon.
  Flashbacks and premonitions / Jon Longhi.
  p. cm.

  1. United States--Social life and customs--20th century--Fiction.
2. Punk culture--United States--Fiction. I. Title.
  PS3562.O4994 F58 1998
  813'.54--dc21

                              98-40166
                              CIP

Contents

FLASHBACKS and PREMONITIONS

PREMONITIONS and FLASHBACKS

It Takes A While For Things To Get Back Home

Veronica got a nose ring. That's no big deal in most places, but it still caused quite a stir with her Uncle Larry when she went back to Kentucky for a family reunion.

He leaned in for a closer inspection and barked, "What the hell is that anti-nosepicking device you have in your face there, little missy?"

What's In A Name?

When I was in Boy Scouts in Virginia there was this guy in my troop named Sonny Samples. One day I was tormenting him horribly about his name.

"Sonny Samples, what kind of a redneck name is that?" I yelled at him. "What did your parents name you after? An episode of *Hee Haw*? That has to be the most hillbilly cracker name I've ever heard in my life. Maybe your parents got your name out of an issue of *Grit* magazine."

On and on, for over a half-hour I kept berating him about what a horrible name he had. Finally I drew to a conclusion.

"But one thing I will say for you," I said, "is that at least you aren't named Junior. Junior Samples would be *the* most redneck name in the universe."

Sonny proceeded to beat the crap out of me. Turns out Junior was his middle name.

A Penny Saved Is A Penny Earned

When we were all little kids my family drove across the country. My sister Melanie was only five at the time. The trip was kind of like a huge connect-the-dots where each dot was a Howard Johnsons. We lived off fried clams and salad bars. At the end of the journey my dad noticed that Melanie had a big bag full of money.

"Where did you get this, sweetheart?" he asked her.

"Well, Daddy," she said. "All the way across the country I noticed that you kept leaving money on the tables. At every restaurant we stopped at you forgot to pick up some of your change. I thought it was really careless so I collected it for you."

My mom tried to feign a sense of moral outrage over the matter for a few minutes but my dad just thought she was a pretty smart kid.

"What the hell," he finally said. "We'll never see those people again anyway."

Car Trouble

My mother often has difficulty recognizing her cars. It's not so much a mental deficiency as severe inattentiveness brought on by her frantic and harried life. Mother is always overbooked. She frequently tries to fit a week's worth of errands into a single day. In a schedule like this, much more than automobiles can be lost. Usually her mind is the first thing to turn up missing. Her stories of stress-based amnesia could fill a clinical psychology textbook but a couple of car incidents stand out from the rest.

One of these occurred when my dad had just gotten out of the hospital after having his appendix removed. He needed pain pills, so Mom went to pick up his prescription at Edgewood Pharmacy. Dad's surgery had taken place during a particularly busy time in her life. She had been out all day running errands and still had to drop the dog off at the vet, pick my sister up from ballet class, drop off the recycling, pick up some groceries, cook dinner, weed the garden, write a letter to her congressman, do the laundry, finish her crossword puzzle, buy some new curtains for the bathroom, drop off old clothes at the church yard sale, and still make it home in time for *Jeopardy* which she watched religiously. To be quite plain, she just didn't have time for my father's illness.

So my mother was in a frantic rush when she sprinted into the pharmacy. At the time, we had two family cars: a big yellow Pontiac sedan and a cobalt blue stationwagon. The prescription took a long time to fill so Mom was already late for picking up my sister from ballet class when she ran out of the drugstore. She leapt through the open door of the yellow Pontiac and whipped out her keys. But something was wrong. The car key wouldn't fit into the ignition. They were definitely the Pontiac keys, not the stationwagon ones, but for some mysterious reason they no longer fit where they were supposed to. As my mother struggled with them she noticed something else. The interior of the car looked slightly odd. The dashboard was altered and she didn't remember that drink holder. Then Mom looked up and saw the three-hundred-pound black woman sitting in the passenger seat. The fat black woman was giving her some kind of a look. "Sorry," my mom said sheepishly. "I thought this was my car."

My mother got out of the yellow Pontiac in complete humiliation. But almost instantly, this feeling was exponentially multiplied because she realized that it hadn't been the yellow Pontiac she had driven to the pharmacy, but the blue stationwagon. So when Mom slunk across the parking lot under the baleful gaze of the humongous woman, she got into a completely different car from the one she had just mistaken for her own.

Another incident of note took place a few years later. By that time my parents were separated, but they still had managed to retain a brittle friendship. Mother was living in an apartment across town from father. He still resided in the house we had grown up in. Mom was working as a jeweler and it was the night before a big crafts show. Like always, Mom was behind in her preparations. Even if she stayed up all night, she still wouldn't be ready to go. So why she offered to cook my Dad a shrimp dinner is anybody's guess. My father had just gotten out of the hospital from back surgery and he was pretty much bedridden, but my mom still could have just picked up some Chinese takeout or had something delivered. There was no need for her to go through the whole time-consuming production of a full home-cooked meal.

She ran into problems immediately. Her car keys were nowhere to be found. My mother scoured every nook and cranny of her apartment for forty-five minutes and still came up empty-handed. So eventually she just decided to use the Hide-A-Key which was tucked behind the front fender in a magnetic box. In those days, my mother was using the big yellow Pontiac sedan and although it was old, it was still fairly reliable. The car had been in a couple of accidents and the chrome strip had been knocked off the side panel, but the engine was still in perfect working order.

Mom went by the fish store and picked up a couple pounds of shrimp, then continued on to the grocery store to get the rest of the ingredients. When she got out of the Pontiac in the supermarket parking lot Mom became paranoid that someone might steal her shrimp so she locked the doors. As soon as she did this she realized her error. The key which she held in her hands was the trunk key, the door key was sitting on the front seat. My mother groaned in helpless frustration.

But all was not lost. There was another set of keys at my father's house. Obviously he couldn't deliver them so my mother called one of her roommates, Tom, who also had a car. About fifteen minutes later he picked her up and they drove to my father's house and got the last set of keys. Mother double-checked to make sure she had the keys to the Pontiac and not the stationwagon.

As soon as Mom and Tom left Dad's house a horrendous winter storm hit. It seemed more like a snow thunderstorm or ice hurricane than a mere blizzard. The town was in the grip of a frigid January and the snowflakes fell so violently that they bounced off the asphalt road. Mom and her roommate slowly made their way through an opaque din of sleet, freezing rain, and whirling white.

By the time they got back to the supermarket there were only a few cars left in the parking lot. They drove up to Mom's car and she got out. My mother had asked Tom to hang out for a few minutes and make sure she got in and got the car started safely.

She went up to the driver's side and stuck her key into the lock. But it wouldn't go in. No matter how Mom jiggled and fiddled it the key refused to fit. 'Damn!' she thought, 'Maybe it's just the lock on this side.' But the lock on the passenger door proved just as unresponsive. Eventually my mother went back to the driver's side but the situation there hadn't changed. The key still wouldn't fit.

"Godammit!" she screamed. "I checked these twice! They have to be the Pontiac keys!"

When another couple of minutes' worth of wiggling and fidgeting still elicited no response, Mom just lost it. She began screaming and kicking the car. Mother pounded it with such violence that she dented in the side panel. It was then that she noticed something strange. The chrome side strip was still there.

'Oh my god,' Mom realized with a sudden horror. 'This isn't my car! It's somebody else's Pontiac!' My mother looked over at her roommate, who sat behind the windshield of his car with an expression of horror and disbelief on his face. Tom seemed to be mentally reassessing whether or not he wanted to live in the same apartment as this crazy woman. Mom just shrugged. "Wrong car!" she yelled to him.

By this time, snow had covered all the cars in the parking lot. So my mother couldn't tell which one was hers. She just ran screaming with her arms up in the air through the buried cars. Eventually she found hers. The keys fit perfectly.

When Mom finally got back to Dad's place, he started screaming at her. "What the hell took you so long?"

"Believe me, Raymond," she said, "you don't want to know."

My mother was really glad that the owner of the abused Pontiac hadn't seen her and called the police. She could already

see the headline in the local paper: CRAZED WOMAN ATTACKS
INNOCENT AUTOMOBILE.

Joe's Lunch

On the boardwalk in Rehoboth Beach was a grimy little lunch counter called Joe's Lunch. It was little more than a hole in the wall, with a smoldering grill and fryer vats which kept an oily atmosphere in the place. Joe's Lunch was no different from any other greasy spoon which dispenses french fries soaked in vinegar and well-done hamburgers to tourists walking on boardwalks up and down the East Coast. The place didn't even have any chairs, just a line of seven barstools along a single counter. The cracked formica you ate off of was so yellow and old it looked like an archaeological find. Few customers were brave enough to use the bathroom which usually doubled as an advertisement for filth. Along the walls, the once happy wallpaper was so dimmed by years of grime that you could hardly make out the original pattern. Mummified flies stuck to it here and there. All the utensils and kitchen fixtures were covered in a charred black layer of burnt grease. There was history in that oil.

Joe, who ran the place, was a hairy little ape of a man. His hominid arms were covered in fur and a riot of chest hair reached up from the collars of his filthy white t-shirts like something that refused to be hidden. Even when he was cleanshaven, his face still wore a five o'clock shadow. Though he was going bald on the top, Joe had so much hair from the neck down that one got the impression that the hair on his scalp had merely sunk into his body and emerged from someplace else.

Joe was always in a surly mood, he would grumble and growl about his grills and fry vats like a caged simian. Physically, he was as ugly as his moods. His face might have looked better if it had worn something besides a scowl, but I wouldn't know, because I never saw him smile. Something about his constantly mean expression let you know that Joe hated every minute of his life and every person who walked in his door. Often when he served you your fries he would tell you how much he loathed you and that he didn't care if you dropped dead after you paid him for the food.

Joe's bedside manner didn't cultivate many repeat customers, but tourists are an unloyal lot. The only customers who ate there on a regular basis were the local punk rockers, of which I was one, and we only dined there because the place had the cheapest fries on the boardwalk. It wasn't the decorum or the ambiance that brought us in. Joe's Lunch was also a good perch from which to watch humanity parade by in all its grotesque splendor. I saw some crazy things go on at that lunch counter.

One of the strangest things I saw was Joe himself. Besides being a restaurateur, he also ran a gay phone sex line through the pay phone next to the counter. Joe did the calls himself, while he was cooking. All the local punks often speculated whether Joe was gay or straight. There were rumors flying around that he had once had sex with a dog.

When he did the phone sex calls, Joe had all kinds of fantasy scenarios. Sometimes he'd play the role of a sugar daddy, or a drag queen, or a young boy. Other times, he pretended to be a black man, a Latin stud, or a male model. And Joe could get real nasty, talking about how the caller on the line was choking his tonsils and how he wouldn't be able to sit down for a week. But no matter what role he was playing, it was always one of a fabulously handsome man, and it was kind of funny watching him standing there with these good-looking stories coming out of the mouth of a hideous little ape in his mid-forties, reeking like a B.O. factory with big circles of perspiration eclipsing the underarms of his greasy white t-shirts.

It was also funny to watch the reactions of the customers. They'd be sitting along the counter stuffing their faces with burgers, fries, and hot dogs. Joe would be slaving over his orders, the drops of sweat spattering as they landed on the food and grill. Suddenly, the pay phone would ring and Joe would walk over and answer it. "Oh, hello Mr. Girth," he'd say. "I've been waiting to feel your big hot salami thrusting up my butt," and then he'd launch into some hot and hunky gay sex monologue right in front of everyone at the counter. All the customers would look down at their food and a slow expression of horror and nausea would spread across their faces.

A Lust For Pumpkin Pie

A friend of mine mailed me an article from a small town newspaper published somewhere near Fresno in the heart of farmland territory. It was a clipping from the local Police Report column. It concerned one Frank Floyd, who had been driving home drunk one night past the farm fields. Now he was not only drunk, but horny as well. The article contained an embarrassed interview with Frank Floyd in jail where he was being held on a charge of lascivious conduct.

"So I was driving past this field of pumpkins," Frank said. "And I thought to myself, 'Well, pumpkins are wet and squishy on the inside.' So I pulled over and walked out into the field until I found a pumpkin that was big, ripe, and just right. It had nice curves. I took out my knife and cut a hole in it, and well... you know... went to it. I figured, hey, I'm not hurting anybody. And besides, I thought no one was around for miles."

But there was someone around. Quite nearby, actually. Police officer Susan Jones saw Frank stumbling around the pumpkin patch and pulled over to investigate a possible trespassing. She was also interviewed in the article.

"I moved up on the subject," she said. "At first stealthily, but then more openly when I ascertained that he was unarmed and intoxicated. He was so busily engaged in his activity that I got up very close to him before he noticed me. I was standing right up over top of him but he was going at it so hard he still didn't notice me. I finally had to say, 'Sir, are you aware you're fucking a pumpkin?'

"The suspect looked up with a start and said, 'Oh! Is it midnight already?'

"I have to admit, in ten years of law enforcement, that's the best snappy comeback line I've heard yet."

Some Things You Wish You Could Forget

We were all at a barbecue and had been eating, drinking, and smoking pot for hours. Eventually the conversation came around to bad acid trips.

At one point, Debbie said to Jason, "That's what you and I have in common, we've both taken off all our clothes in front of large groups of people while we were on lots of drugs."

"That may be," Jason said. "But they were two totally different experiences. Yours was a positive, life-affirming thing. Mine was profoundly negative.

"To begin with, I was in L.A. I was tripping with some friends and we were walking along one of those interminable palm-lined avenues. This windowpane we'd dropped was so kickass it could've made Tim Leary see God.

"What was it exactly that set me off? Oh, I remember. My friend Joe threw his tennis shoe at me. I thought it was some kind of a game where the weapons you used were clothes. So I started throwing my clothes at him. Only I went a bit overboard and threw everything I was wearing at Joe. So I found myself naked in the middle of the street. I just remember standing in my bare feet on this manhole cover, this circle inside a square made by the white lines of the crosswalks. I was the center of the universe and all around me these roads were radiating off into the distance with crowds of people along the sides of them, black people, white people, yellow people, brown people, a lush spectrum of rainbow humans and they're all pointing at me and getting in an uproar. I was flabbergasted at their reaction.

" 'What's wrong with you all!' I started screaming. 'Why are you so fucking uptight!? This is California! This is California!' "

CaFFeiNe CoNFidaNte

There's a bum on Haight Street who's always camped out at the same place on the sidewalk next to this Mexican restaurant. He sits on a couple of milk crates. In front of him is another stack of milk crates which acts as a kind of altar for his coffee cup. His coffee cup is the bum's best friend. He talks to the cup of joe as if it's a real person.

One night, me and my friend Lisa were getting ready to go to dinner down the block. We were in front of the entrance when a couple of yuppies walked past the bum who was deep in conversation with his coffee cup. The tramp suddenly looked up and began screaming the most violent profanities at them.

"Get off the street, you fuckwads!" he yelled. "You're polluting the atmosphere."

Then he turned towards us. Me and Lisa braced ourselves for the attack.

"Don't worry," the bum said. "I'm not mad at you. I asked my coffee cup about you, and according to him, you two are okay."

A Case OF Mistaken Identity

The corner of Haight and Ashbury is constantly swarming with acid and weed dealers whispering, "Buds... Doses," to people passing by. These friends of mine live at 666 Ashbury which is just a few doors down from the corner and they are well aware of the situation. One night while sitting around drinking they decided as a prank to develop a personality, an artificial resident who would be the recipient of huge amounts of junk mail. They named their creation Bud Doses.

They started with the late night 800 number commercials. The residents of 666 called every one they saw. Especially the ads with free giveaways. Bud got everything they had to give. Information packets. Free videos. Catalogues and a flood of junk mail. Thigh Master demonstration tapes, Soloflex pamphlets, get rich quick schemes. Bud's interests fleshed out and he became a well-rounded individual.

But they didn't stop there. They signed Bud up for the Publishers Clearinghouse Sweepstakes. He joined fan clubs. Got twelve records for a dollar. Bud applied for credit cards. Identification papers. He put in phone calls to late night TV lawyers asking them to help him with crimes which had never occurred. The residents of 666 signed Bud up for every contest and grand prize giveaway that crossed their path. They were even tempted to buy him a lottery ticket. But what if he won?

By spring, the residents of 666 had collected so much mail for Bud Doses that they had wallpapered an entire room with envelopes addressed to him. They figured he was working out so well that they should expand, branch him out and share him with other people on the block. So they began sending junk mail for Bud to all of their neighbors. Mr. Doses had multiple addresses. He was everywhere. Soon the corner surged with a junk mail flood as thick as the dealers who swarmed around the sidewalks. And still nobody knew exactly who Bud was. Judging from the amount of mail he got you'd figure he was the most popular guy in town. But you can't always measure someone just by their correspondence and who they associate with. Who was the real Bud Doses? We'll probably never know. Perhaps it was all just a case of mistaken identity, the mistake being that so many people thought Bud actually had an identity.

That summer the inevitable finally occurred. Someone actually came to the front door of 666 looking for the mystery man. They wanted to meet him in person. It turned out that Bud had won a year's supply of invisible ink from one of the many contests he had entered. A representative from the ink company had come by with two gallons of the clear liquid and was very anxious to meet the big winner and take his picture. The residents of 666 were deliberately vague about Bud's whereabouts. Soon the invisible ink representative realized he was being stalled and got a little hot under the collar.

"Listen," he said petulantly, "I'm tired of being given the runaround. Now I want to know right now: Where is Bud Doses?"

"Well, he's kinda neither here nor there," one of the roommates said. "Always on the move, you know. One of those people who's everywhere and nowhere at the same time. In fact, as far as we're concerned, there's a little bit of Bud Doses in all of us."

New Leaf

In high school, Frankie mowed lawns. A few years later he'd expanded his lawnmowing operations and had two people working for him. Eventually it became a full-grown business and he had tractors and leafblowers. He had municipal contracts. Every summer he raked it in, so to speak.

Frankie had smoked pot for the past fifteen years and at times he had a problem with it. Ever since he'd had money, Frankie had a fat bag and was always in search of the bottom of it. But he was older now. He had a wife and kid. Had probably become a Christian. Frankie felt it was time to straighten up his life. Quit that shit.

One day he was driving around the Delaware back roads getting stoned because that's all there is to do in Delaware. Frankie looked down at the big bag of weed on his lap. 'You know,' he thought, 'if I smoke this bag down to the bottom I'll just go out and buy another. But if I have the strength to just pour it out right now I might be able to quit smoking pot.' So Frankie rolled down his window and began dumping out his weed. Unfortunately, he was so wrapped up in the momentous profundity of this moment that he wasn't paying attention to the road and ran through a stop sign. Of course, a cop happened to be right there. The officer pulled Frankie over and busted him for possession of marijuana.

"Did you tell the cop what you were doing?" I had to ask. "That you were in the process of quitting?"

"No," Frankie said sadly. "What cop would ever believe a story like that? And can you blame them? I just sat there shaking my head in my hands."

Bodiless Profession

I sell books to bookstores. Everyday I sit at the same stationary desk in the same city, but through the miracle of Alexander Graham Bell's discovery my voice travels thousands of miles around the country in the course of an eight-hour shift. Being a phone salesman is a bodiless profession because you seldom meet your customers in the flesh. One of my favorite retail accounts is Tin Boot, an anarchist bookstore in Milwaukee. For somewhere around fifteen years now, this one guy, Phillip, has been the manager and bookbuyer there. I've been selling him books for the past five and have gotten to know him quite well in a long distance sense. I would consider him a friend, and during our phone conversations we have had long discussions of philosophy, politics, and the general state of affairs on our respective sides of the country. He keeps me posted on the Milwaukee scene, I provide updates from California. But it is a completely disembodied relationship which exists entirely through the phone. He was out visiting San Francisco for two weeks and we got together for lunch.

Before moving to California I lived in the Midwest. I had met Phillip a couple times at Tin Boot back in Milwaukee when I used to shop there years ago, but I didn't really get to know him until I lived in California. It had been so long since I had seen him that I forgot what he looked like. Phillip turned out to be tall, thin and wiry, with a scraggly beard growing like lichen on his chin. His whole appearance was one of undernourishment.

We went out to a little Mexican place down the street, right in the heart of the Mission. Phillip is a strict vegetarian, just like a good anarchist. He referred to his trip as the Sex Tour 94. Phillip is gay and he had been sampling some of the more exotic local men's clubs. Nude hot tubs, erotic massage, buddy booths, the whole nine yards. Over our food we talked about philosophy, politics, writers, the weather. After awhile I brought the conversation around to a question I'd been meaning to ask.

"Now I know you don't make your living just from the store," I said. "There's not enough money in books."

"No," Phillip replied. "The store's purely volunteer."

"Then how do you make ends meet?" I asked. "Pay the rent? What do you do for a day job?"

Phillip looked at me in a way which let me know that what he was about to tell me was serious and true. "People don't believe me when I tell them this. But basically, I suck my own dick to make a living."

"How do you mean?" I asked.

"I suck my own dick. I can do it. And people pay me money to do it in private shows. In fact, my whole trip out here is sponsored by five private performances at these sex parties. And I'll go back to Milwaukee with money in my pocket."

I must have had some kind of a look on my face. "I don't know whether to be shocked or jealous," I said. "You don't mind if I quickly duck my head under the table to verify your story, do you?"

Phillip chuckled. "It's just this talent I have," he said. "I've been able to do it since puberty and finally found a way to make money with it. A lot of the cash comes from videos. The first two I did myself. Made my own sets, set the camera up and then filmed myself doing this. Some of the later videos were more professional. I put a little ad in the back of gay porno mags and get mail orders for them. Sell enough to clear a couple thousand dollars and then I quit working for a few months. See, I can live on next to nothing. I only pay $150 a month in rent. We're talking Wisconsin, it's not S.F., or New York. So because of this little talent, I've been able to avoid a regular job for over ten years now."

Personally, I don't care about how he makes his living, but I do worry about Phillip. I mean, what if some day his talent gives out? What if it shrinks, or he can't get turned on by himself anymore? How will he make a living? Phillip is smart enough to get a good job, but what if they quiz him about past work experience? "What have you been doing for the past ten years?" Will he truthfully describe his self-sucking abilities on a resumé?

I was talking to Sam Silent about this when he revealed that he could suck himself off, too. This ability is more common than you would think.

"I could only suck my own dick when I was very young," I said. "I'm double-jointed, and back when I was really limber I could just reach the tip of my penis. The only problem was, by that point, the pretzel-like position I was in was excruciatingly uncomfortable. My spine was so curved around that I was in serious pain. Plus I had to really stretch my dick out a lot, and when it got hard, it wouldn't reach my mouth anymore."

"I had the same problem," Sam said. "Only with me it was something deeper. More psychological. Like, I like getting my cock sucked. But I don't like sucking cock. I mean, I don't mind eating pussy, but I don't like sucking dick. I'm pretty much straight. So the combined homosexual implications of sucking my own cock got so weird that the whole thing just turned me off."

"That's something to think about," I said. "If you're a guy and you have sex with yourself, you're still technically having sex with a guy. So every time a guy masturbates, it's actually a homosexual act."

"Exactly!" Sam exclaimed. "But I only seemed to realize this when I had my own cock in my mouth."

Dada's Penis Pipe

That summer was a dry one for potheads in Delaware. The War on Drugs was in full effect and you could find nary a roach through two weeks of desperate pleading phone calls, calling in every old favor, all the dealers didn't even have head stash. There was plenty of cocaine available, in fact people were already beginning to die from it but if you wanted the mellow weed you were hard-pressed to find even a seed. Yet my friend Dada Trash managed to keep a connection all through that long sober August.

Over the course of the month he hooked us up with three tolerable quarter-ounces of sinse. The major problem though was that if you were at a party and wanted to catch a buzz, the odor of a joint soon electrified the clearheaded crowd with the same hungry interest one sees in schools of sharks who have just swum through a cloud of blood. Before we were up to three puffs, we would find ourselves surrounded by hulking high school jocks and drooling dirtball rednecks who had suddenly become our best friends. If we passed the joint on, it never came back, and sometimes the jocks would get so desperate for us to share it they'd threaten to beat us up if we didn't. Situations like this are bad enough without them being connected to a drug that already makes you paranoid.

After a number of tense social scenes at a couple of parties Dada Trash came up with a novel solution to our dilemma. He bought a ten-inch-long rubber penis from a sex shop on Route 13 and put a bowl in it. The dildo was completely lifelike, hollow, and airtight. A pipe bowl was back between the balls and on the end where the pee hole was Dada drilled a tiny opening you had to suck through.

After that, when we were at parties and somebody asked, "Hey, you got any pot?" Dada Trash would say, "Sure," and whip out his bag. The person would yell, "COOL!" and already a crowd would be forming. Then Dada Trash would whip out the dick bowl and say, "But we have to use my pipe."

Instantly the rednecks' and jocks' heads would snap back and they'd reflexively hold their hands up in front of their faces like he'd pulled out a turd or something. They'd be offering to let us use every bong in the house, saying things like, "Don't you think that pot would taste better in my special rolling papers which look like an American flag?" or "Wouldn't you prefer a tokemaster?" but me and Dada Trash remained firm in our choice of conduits. And we'd stick that big rubber dick in our mouths and smoke bowl after bowl all night long right in the middle of the crowd.

Of course, we were more than willing to share and kept offering people a hit, sometimes going so far as to jab the pipe at their faces with an almost conjugal gesture. But hardly anyone ever accepted. The rednecks and jocks would look at us with scowling faces and clenched fists. Sometimes they'd get so frustrated they'd yell out, "How come you won't smoke out of anything else?"

Dada Trash would just smile as he took a big hit. "I like this pipe," he'd say while exhaling. "It just tastes better."

TWo PeaS IN A PoD

Mary had two uncles who were brothers. Both of them left their wives to be in a homosexual relationship with each other. They moved to San Francisco and have been lovers ever since.

"It's a real topic of conversation at family reunions," Mary told us. Last night me and Len were telling this story to our friend, Maria.

"I keep looking for these guys everywhere around town. These two middle-aged queens who look really similar to each other," Len said.

"Oh, that reminds me of these two uncles of my friend, Sara," Maria said. "They're gay twin brothers who live together in some rural town in New Hampshire and the two of them carve wooden ducks for a living. One of them can carve any species of duck in any pose. But the other just carves the same duck over and over. He's carved the same duck over and over now for more than twenty years."

SNOOdLINg ANd SNarFLINg

Dada Trash told me about some wild sex practice called snoodling. It's where a man fucks another man in the penis. I guess one guy fucks the other in the foreskin or something. There have been reports in the local sex advice columns that some men have had their urethras surgically enlarged so they can have other men fuck them in their penises. Their genitals are both convex and concave at the same time.

Thor told me about goobering. That's where one person farts in a bathtub and the other person bites the bubbles.

Dada Trash recently thought up a new sex practice called snarfling. It's where you stick a straw in your butt, put the other end in another man's anus and fart into his colon. Then through the straw, you suck your own fart out of another man's ass.

I think Dada Trash has a little too much spare time on his hands these days.

Shop Talk

Today at work, this woman came in from some place called Fetish World. It's an erotica store for sophisticated adults. I work at a book and magazine distributor. A lot of what we sell is porno.

"So what's the deal on this whole branding craze?" the woman from Fetish World asked. "I saw a lot about it in the kink magazines, papers, and literature there for a couple months, but now it seems to have faded away. I thought it was going to be the next big thing after piercing."

"I don't know," I said. "Maybe people just realized that it hurts."

"And I'll bet you thought the whole piercing and modern primitive scene would just progress through more extreme forms of mutilation till people worked their way up to amputations," Sam Silent put in.

"I always thought that ritualistic amputation could put the hop back into the hip hop scene," I quipped.

Then the lady from Fetish World started telling us about some book we carry called *The Horseman: Confessions of A Zoophile*. She had just finished reading it. It is the touching, true life tale of a man who has sex with horses. When I sell *The Horseman* to people I tell them it gives new meaning to the phrase "Ride 'em, cowboy." But I've never actually read the book.

"So does he make love to male or female horses?" I asked.

"Oh, female horses," she replied blithely.

"Yeah, what do you think he is, some kind of a pree-vert or something?" Sam belted out in a good ole boy accent.

Brick House

When I first moved to the city I started hanging out with this girl who had horrible sex problems. She didn't have problems getting picked up, it's just that guys would only sleep with her once and then never speak to her again. She was a real slut. It was like she thought she was some kind of vixen or sex kitten and she'd always dress up in these tight leather outfits and rubber halters, wearing high-heeled stiletto pumps and things. She was a big blond German girl, must have been almost six feet tall. Her name was Britta Wall, but because she was a large girl everyone called her Brick Wall. Her family name had been Vul but they changed it to Wall when they moved to America. Anyway, Brick lived with me and Sara when we moved into our first apartment in the city.

Whenever we all went out, Brick just had to pick some guy up. She was so aggressive. She'd walk up to a complete stranger in a club and go, "How would you like to have your cock sucked?" If you want to pick a guy up that's a pretty effective opening line.

I remember one night a bunch of us came back to our apartment from this disco. It was six girls and this one ugly guy who Brick wanted to pick up and we were all kinda drunk. We're hanging out in the living room and Brick puts on this record of Joan Jett and The Blackhearts singing "I Wanna Be Your Dog" and disappears into the next room. A couple of minutes later she comes out wearing just her panties, wobbling on these cherry red high-heels and she's all wrapped up in an American flag. Then she starts doing a slow bump and grind striptease in front of everyone in the room. But we could tell it was all focused at this one ugly guy. She's coming up to him, rubbing herself all over his jeans and stuff and he's so freaked out that he just starts talking really quickly and nervously to all the other girls in the room who have their clothes on. Only, he was trying to pick all the girls up. He's asking if they want to go to bed with him while this nude woman is rubbing her sweaty body all over his jeans. Finally, later that night Brick and him slept together, but it was another of her one-day affairs.

And it's funny. She didn't have to act like that. Brick was a really pretty girl. She was big, but she had a great figure and a beautiful face with high cheekbones and blue eyes. I don't know. Maybe she just had no self-respect.

The worst was one night when we were at this speed metal club. Brick picked up some vampire leather guy. He was pretty though, with a smooth girlish face and long dyed black hair. But it was her typical routine. After five minutes of shouting over the band he just coldly asks, "Your place or mine?"

"Yours," she said, which was stupid because a girl should never go home with some guy she just met in a bar. At least not to his place. Well, anyway, they go out to his apartment in the Sunset district. It's a huge luxury flat, incredibly expensive place, and he lives there all alone. For awhile they sit around doing some coke in front of the TV. Then he gets up and goes into the bedroom and closes the door and leaves her sitting there in the living room watching TV. For a few minutes she waits for him to come out but it soon becomes apparent that he's not going to. So she gets up and goes into the bedroom. It's a huge room with two big double beds in the center, side by side, about two or three feet apart from each other. He's taken off his clothes and is lying spoon-style in the left hand one, pretending to be asleep. Brick calls out his name but he doesn't answer. So she takes off her clothes and gets into the right hand bed. For awhile they lay there in their separate beds and Brick listens to the clock tick, waiting for him to come over and join her. But he just stays there, completely still, pretending to be asleep. So eventually Brick gets up and joins him in the left hand bed. She starts rubbing her breasts and body against his back but he won't roll over and face her. Finally, he reaches back, grabs her knee, and starts rubbing it against his bottom. Then he pulls his ass cheeks open and starts shoving her knee up his butt. And he starts talking in a falsetto voice, going, "Oh yeah, boy, shove it into me, make my pussy wet." His whole personality just shifts into the feminine as he shoves her knee into his ass harder and faster until he comes while squealing out these high-pitched moans. Then he falls right to sleep without even turning over to face her.

Brick had another weird sexual problem. Most people thought she had four breasts. When she wore tight clothing it looked like she had a little lower pair below her regular boobs. But they weren't really tits. She just had these unnaturally large ribs. Plus she was skinny, so they stuck out even further. But they caused her real embarrassment on a number of occasions. One time she was making out with this guy who was kind of drunk and he started feeling up her chest, only the things he settled into concentrating on were her big ribs, not what was above them. He was going to town, and finally she just had to look down and say, "Those are not my tits."

PerMaNeNt DaMage

Dada Trash told me about a hooker he saw in London. She was a punk rocker type who was all skanked out on something strong. FUCK YOU was tattooed on her cheek. It was obvious she had done the tattoo by herself with a mirror when she was all fucked up because it was done in an uneven scrawl and FUCK YOU was spelled backwards.

Keith recently met this tattoo artist at a party. He asked the woman if anybody had ever requested a tattoo that she refused to do for anything other than obvious health reasons. Yes, there had been. One time a guy came into the shop who wanted a tattoo across his forehead that read: Look At Me, I Have A Small Penis.

This guy walked into the head shop I was working at a few years ago. He was a piece of complete white trash from Maryland. Had on a Lynyrd Skynyrd t-shirt and his breath reeked of Jack Daniels. The tattoo covered most of his forearm. It looked like a homemade tattoo with those jerky freehand drawn letters that someone must have done with a ballpoint pen, sewing needle, and a bottle of India ink. There was no illustration, just the personal statement: I LOVE DRUGS.

PINOCCHIO'S DreaMS

Pinocchio was a doll who dreamed wooden dreams. Sometimes all he remembered was splinters of them, but he hung on to these like a freezing man clutching his last matchsticks in the frozen North. You see, Pinocchio loved his dreams, they were the only place no strings were attached. Not like real life, where somebody was always jerking him this way and that.

He may have been made of wood, but Pinocchio still had to go out and work to keep a roof over his head, just like everyone else. If he was to stay out in the rain he risked coming down with a bad case of rot. So Pinocchio had to pay the rent.

Not too many people wanted to hire a puppet, and even when he got a job they usually fired him after a couple of days because he was too short or uncoordinated or something. Their reasons for terminating him were vague at best. It was outright discrimination and Pinocchio knew it, but what could he do? He didn't have the money to fight a court case or the time and connections to start a political action party of vaudeville dolls which could lobby and get an equal rights law for puppets passed. So poor little Pinocchio got by as best he could.

Soon his endless bouts of unemployment drove him to drink. But the poison he chose was even stronger than the highest proof whiskey. Pinocchio did shots of straight shellac as he wasted away the afternoons and nights in sleazy skid row bars, clinging to their shadows like a big wooden mushroom.

And his lies kept getting him into trouble. Often they led to barroom brawls, and if it weren't for the fact that it had been broken off three or four times, his nose would have been six feet long. Pinocchio was addicted to lying. He just couldn't stop himself. Fibs would germinate in his brain, and in a matter of minutes grow out through his mouth like redwoods spreading their branches into full grown tall tales.

Pinocchio had no control over them. He tried twelve-step programs, slander detoxes, even religion. Nothing worked. Right before his last therapist quit, he suggested that Pinocchio should just accept the untruths as incurable and learn to live with them. The shrink advised the puppet to pursue a career in politics. On the few occasions when he was honest with himself, Pinocchio admitted that lying was his only real talent. "If only my dick got bigger every time I told a lie," the little doll would lament to himself. "At least then I could get work as a porno star."

One night in the cigarette haze of Dirty Dave's Down and Out Pub Pinocchio heard some scurvy toothless mouth say, "In L.A. people will lie to you just because they're practicing to lie to someone more important."

That sentence struck Pinocchio's brain like a revelation. He knew he'd discovered his homeland. A place where he could fit in. The next day he moved to the City Of Angels.

Pinocchio went on to make millions as a lie counselor. His TV infomercials, videotapes, and one to one training sessions with CEOs, politicians, and other leaders of industry taught them to be better liars. He gave seminars on Advanced Deception, How to Lie to the Media, Slander as a Hobby, and How to Falsify Your Books. Pinocchio was a lie coach and everybody wanted him on their team. Soon the doll was charging a thousand dollars an hour for private sessions.

Eventually the puppet's reputation as an expert in the Science of Untruths became so great that he was asked to run a presidential campaign. After all, the United States was a country where professional liars made six-figure salaries as spin doctors. That wooden doll was a natural. All of his dreams came true - money, fame, power. He was number one in his field, *Time* magazine voted him Liar Of The Year. Pinocchio's motto was, "If someone tells you I'm the best, I'll deny it." Of course, he had to shell out a lot of money to plastic surgeons and carpenters to keep his nose problem under control, but in the long run, that was a small price to pay for all he had gained. Pinocchio's lies had truly served up the American Dream.

Clues For the Clueless

Everyone at this party was either involved with alternative newspapers or the zine underground. Definitely a get-together of stimulating conversations. Armchair anarchists out the wazoo, self-publishing eccentrics, fringe dwellers, I even met a couple of bonafide crackpots. One of these was the penultimate lefty anarchist. In his mid-forties, long grey hair in a ponytail, ex-hippie wearing John Lennon glasses. He was manic, jittery, and spit out a ceaseless stream of conversation like a ticker tape.

"These anarchist kids today, always whining and complaining," he said. "They just have no creativity. Like with the fake Fast Passes situation. So you wanna ride the busses for free? Man, I bootlegged those things for years. So they have a holographic strip on them now. Easy. You just go out and buy some holographic foil. They sell the shit for about three dollars a square foot. You slice off a ribbon and stick it on a color xerox. If anything, the foil will make your fakes look even more legitimate. So a Muni driver catches you every now and then, what can he do? Kick you off his bus? Just wait for the next one to come along and use your fake Fast Pass to get on it.

"And all these zine publishers complaining about the price of postage. Go out and have a rubber stamp made for about nine bucks that says: US Postage Paid. Works ninety-eight percent of the time. Some organization I worked for back in '70s had one of those and it paid for all our mail for a decade.

"Now the BART train is a little tougher to crack. Those metallic strips on the back of the card can be problematic till you realize how cheap the transit authorities are. It's just a strip of regular cassette tape. In fact, if you've got an old tape player you can run that plastic card through the heads and hear what the code is. All you need is a computer with a sound program, hook it up to the tape player, run the BART card through the heads, and have the computer record and save the code. Then you print out the code onto sections of cassette tape by hooking your computer up to a four-track, cut the tape into strips and paste them onto a piece of plastic. Boom, instant access to BART, wherever you want to go, just slide your plastic through the slot in the turnstiles and watch them open up. Now it doesn't take a rocket scientist to figure this shit out. Anybody with a rudimentary computer audio program can do it. The guy who taught me did it for years well, but they busted him, sent him up river. Course he was printing up fake BART cards ten thousand at a time."

It turns out that the person who had taught him all this was an underground legend known as Captain Crunch. The Captain earned his nickname when he discovered that a giveaway whistle in boxes of Captain Crunch cereal could be used to crack long distance calling codes. Most telecommunication companies coordinate their long distance calls with a series of tones. The Captain discovered that if you blew one of these little plastic whistles into the receiver the computer would mistake it for the access tone and give you free long distance. Needless to say, when word of this hit the street, sales of the sugar-sweetened cereal skyrocketed. Even once the toy giveaway was discontinued, the whistles were still traded in the underground black market. This was but one of dozens of pranks and scams Captain

Crunch had pulled off for fun and profit. But you can only fuck the government and corporations for so long before they send in their big guns. Evidently the Captain had been brought up on a number of federal charges and served some serious jail time over the years.

Through the evening I met a number of these people, drifting around the apartment from one countercultural intellectual conversation to another. Vegans, libertarians, obscure collectors, political queers, aficionados of psychedelic poster art, polemicists, ranters and ravers all. The whole time building a comfortable buzz on imported beers and Humboldt bud. In the back room some underground types got me bookoo stoned. I asked them, "Are you all zine people or newspaper people?" They answered, "We're hangers-on to the zine scene." Xerox groupies. After the green had done its rounds they fell into a conversation about snack foods. Each of them giving lurid descriptions of their favorite brands of cookies, potato chips, snack cakes and Moon Pies, and I thought, Are these people mindless stoners or what?

Heads Up

I work with a woman named Virus who comes from a nocturnal terrain of Haight Street casualties. Every day she shows up for work at 4:30. Vampire shift. Her hair is a tangled mess of dreadlocks spraypainted green. She's a witch, practices various arcane rituals, believes in dark gods. Her name used to be Iris, but she changed it to Virus to fit her new lifestyle. Or deathstyle. Often her opinions and tastes are lucid and quite good. But she's completely insane. Her friends are a drug-addled Addams Family. Goth death rockers who read too much Manson and Wilhelm Reich. Pictures of Aleister Crowley hang on their black walls above melted candles.

One of Virus's friends was moving recently and had a yard sale to unload some stuff. Only the sale got him into trouble with the police because out there on the blanket with his lava lamps and old Bauhaus records was his collection of fetuses in jars of formaldehyde. Their pale withered bodies looking sad among the other cluttered junk. Two beat cops arrested him. They weren't even exactly sure what to charge him with. When Virus was describing this to me she said, "Now, almost everybody I know has a fetus in a jar, at least a human hand or body part, but everyone knows you're not supposed to sell them on the street!"

When I walked into work Monday the first thing I heard my boss Don say was, "You know, I had a friend who once traded a six-legged calf for a severed head in a jar."

He was talking to his lawyer. I guess discussions of litigation often lead one's thoughts to realms of grimoire.

"When I was living in this hippie crash pad up in the Haight," Don continued, "we used to set the head up on the table during Thanksgiving dinner."

"Was that because it was the head of the house?" I asked.

"We just didn't want it to feel left out," Don snickered. "When I first moved in, the jar was full of formaldehyde but by the time I moved out the liquid had all drained away and the head was dried up and mummified.

"Speaking of death stories, when I was back in Fresno, me and a friend of mine were riding past this field when a plane crashed in it. We pulled over and ran out to check the wreckage. Found the pilot's helmet and his head was still in it."

"Pretty grisly," the lawyer sighed. And that from the mouth of a lawyer, I thought.

"Not only that," said Don, "but afterwards, me and my friend got into a fight over who would get to keep the helmet and whether or not we could use it again."

"I guess it depended on which of you wanted to be a redhead," I quipped.

That Friday when I walked into work the first thing I heard Don say was, "I guess you heard about Fred Rollins?"

"No," I said.

"He got busted on Tuesday," Don replied. "Cops raided his house and popped him for cultivation. They also confiscated his head. The papers got ahold of the story, and the *Chronicle* headline was: POT BUST UNCOVERS SEVERED HEAD."

"Don," I said, "that wasn't *the* head was it?"

"Yeah, it was," Don said. "Rollins traded Wilson a six-legged goat for it back in the '60s. He's had it ever since. It's funny, this all happened the day after I told you that story. Some snitch turned him in. I called up Fred and got the lowdown on the dude. He's a real creep. One of these Berkeley lowlifes who's a borderline homeless person. All of his front teeth are black, some kind of rot or something. Guy's spent a few years in the joint, evidently he got out by informing on people. Anyway, that's how he makes his living now, he's a career snitch. The Berkeley police pay him every time he turns in a grower. And he hangs out in that community, the old hippie pot-smoking Telegraph Ave crowd, looking for people. He'd been to a party at Fred's house so that's how he knew Rollins had the head. But the pot... evidently the snitch was getting stoned with some hippie woman on the roof of Fred's building. He looked down through a skylight and there on the piano was Fred's one pot plant. Two hours later the cops had searched Fred's apartment and booked him. They probably wouldn't have made a big deal about the head but evidently there was some guy they busted in the city about a month ago who was selling a bunch of fetuses in jars at a yard sale and the cops were afraid that things like this were becoming a prevalent problem."

My world gets ever smaller and more circular.

THe PerFect EMPLoyee

I've been married for a couple of years now, but many of my male friends are still single. Hanging out with the boys helps keep me sane and married, but I'm glad I'm not one of the boys full time anymore. The other night I was hanging out with two of my old pals, Lefty Frith and Matt Walker, or "M" as he calls himself these days. From the sound of the tales those two boys were telling, the single world of dating is no picnic. Both of them have been on one dud date after another. But by far the worst tale came from Matt.

He met these two girls in a bar and fell into talking with them. After a few minutes, he seemed to be hitting it off pretty well with a girl named Gail. Gail worked out of her apartment and had an office set up in her living room. She only had one employee, who was a combination of accountant, bookkeeper, and secretary. Like most small business owners, Gail had trouble finding qualified help.

"You wouldn't believe how substandard some of the people I've hired have been," Gail bemoaned. "Just because someone was a good bike messenger doesn't mean I'm about to put them in charge of my financial records. Even when I got somebody who worked out, they'd inevitably quit after a couple days. So I was overjoyed when Francine applied. At first I was a little curious, because she was tremendously overqualified. Had a Masters in Economics, loads of experience. I mean, why did she want to work for someone like me? She could be pulling in ten times as much downtown. But Francine was too good to pass up. I hired her on the spot.

"And she was all I could ever have hoped for in an employee. Always on time, intelligent, pleasant, organized. She's kept flawless books and has a wonderful personality.

"There's only one problem. Today I came in, and she had taken a dump in the middle of the office."

"What do you mean?" M asked.

"I mean she took a shit on the carpet," Gail explained. "Right next to the xerox machine."

"I mean, why?" M asked. "Was there an argument?"

"No," Gail continued. "No explanation. Just dropped her drawers and squatted in the middle of the office and relieved herself. Completely out of the blue. For no apparent reason whatsoever. Francine seemed as shocked and surprised about the whole thing as I was. In fact, that's one of the reasons I'm out drinking tonight. I just can't figure out how I should handle the whole situation."

M and her talked for another hour or so and exchanged phone numbers. A couple weeks later, they went out on a date.

During the course of the date, M commented, "That was a pretty crazy story you told me about that woman who took a dump in your office."

"Oh that!" Gail said. "You know, it's funny you should mention it, because Francine took another shit next to my desk today."

"Again?!" M exclaimed.

"Yep," Gail answered.

"Why didn't you fire her after she did it the first time?" M asked incredulously.

"I just couldn't," Gail explained. "You don't know how hard it is to find good help these days. Francine is the most intelligent and hard-working employee I've ever had. I mean, except for that one little idiosyncrasy, her job performance has been flawless."

"Flawless maybe, but it sure hasn't been spotless," M said.

Bad Night At The Chameleon
For Kurt and Bucky

It was a hot night. I mean, a real hot night. We have nights like that, even in San Francisco. Most of the year it's room temperature, but once or twice a year we get one of those scorcher days that's as sweaty and uncomfortable as anything a humidity-drenched East Coast August can serve up. And because the people in San Francisco are used to such good weather they really can't handle days like this.

As soon as I walked into the club everyone in the place looked angry. They were sitting there at the bar throwing them down in such a way that you knew things weren't going good in their lives. Doing shots like the glass was full of rattlesnake venom. Now you know what kind of a place the Chameleon is, don't you? Those people are animals. They're a rough bunch, a tough crowd. Rumor has it that the Chameleon poetry readings are the roughest in the country.

Man, people come from all over the country, and all the counties around San Francisco, just to get heckled there. In literary circles, it's like a rite of passage. Like one night these girls from the suburbs were there reading this bad love poetry and people started heckling them, and they just started smiling like it was this big honor to be booed.

Well, this was the angriest crowd I've ever seen at the Chameleon. They were downright ornery. The featured reader wasn't helping things because she gave this furious reading, all this angst-ridden revolutionary stuff that had the whole crowd stirred up. They were yelling along with her. People were shaking their fists up in the air, and then the open reading started. And people were pissed, everyone was reading their angriest shit, and if the audience didn't like it, they'd tear the person on stage to shreds. The crowd wanted blood.

About the tenth person on stage was this old homeless hippie guy. He was a short withered-up specimen of '60s optimism who had experienced some serious chemical brain damage along the way. Beneath a dirty, smudged Cat In The Hat tophat billowed long stringy blonde hair. He wore a faded and tattered jean jacket with a peace sign on the back which had been cut out of an American flag and sewed on in what was obviously a drunken and late night manner. The aura of grayness about his pants led me to believe he had not washed them in a good two months. That and the fact that he smelled like rotten bananas.

He read this horrible rhyming poem which kept comparing women's vaginas to sewer openings in the gutter. Well, of course that went over like a lead balloon. About a third of the room was bald-headed dykes with all these piercings hanging out of their faces, and they started screaming, "Get off the stage! Get off the stage!" Soon the chant was picked up by the whole crowd just for the hell of it, to torment the guy. They weren't there to listen, they were there to provoke. But the hippie kept on reading through all the catcalls, and boos and hisses even though the yells for him to get off the stage were so loud you couldn't hear what he was reading anymore. His poem lasted a couple minutes.

The policy at the Chameleon is one poem or five minutes. Now Homeless Hippie Guy had done his one poem, but he didn't want to leave the stage yet. He also wanted to play this song he had written on an old beat-up acoustic guitar strung around his neck. Well, when he tried to do this, the crowd just exploded.

"Get off the stage!" they screamed, or, "One piece!"

Someone screamed, "Bucky! Get him off stage!" The rest of the crowd agreed and started yelling their support for this idea.

Bucky sheepishly walked up on stage. "Look, dude," he said. "The rules say you can only read one poem. You'll have to get off."

"Five minutes!" the little homeless guy yelled. "The rules say I get five minutes."

"One poem!" the audience screamed. "Get him off!"

Everyone's temperature was as hot as the thick air in that room. The hippie tried to just start into his song, some light little ditty about peace, love and happiness or some other bullshit, but he was singing it real aggressively, like no one's going to get him off that stage till he's done with it. Bucky walked up and put his hand on the guy's shoulder.

And the hippie turns around and slugs him! Bucky's glasses go flying. He's like, "What the fuck!" He can't see. And the little guy hits him again. Now Bucky's no little dude, so he pops the bum in the face and then grabs him in this big bear hug, but the little guy keeps squirming around, trying to get away.

At that point the bartender clears the bar. He's a big dude, about six foot four, over two hundred pounds. And he runs up and starts punching the fuck out of this guy's face. The bartender's fists looked like big ham hocks or sides of beef pounding him.

He was brutalizing him. By this point, the bartender had opened up his face and blood was exploding everywhere, yet the little homeless guy still kept screaming and struggling to get free. So the bartender threw him off the stage. He went flying through the air and then Bam! landed face first on this chair and flattened it right there. Just collapsed the whole thing.

I was just a couple of tables back in the crowd. This happened right in front of my face. I figured the fall had put his lights out. Bucky walked up to see if he was okay. And the dude jumped up and attacked him! He still wasn't out. I mean, this guy had just flattened a metal chair with his face and he still wanted to fight. It was like one of those zombie movies where they keep coming back from the dead.

I'd had a couple of drinks' worth of courage so I started to get up to help Bucky fight the guy. I was like, what the hell, let's get it on, have a brawl, yeah! But my girlfriend grabs my arm and says sternly, "Don't you get involved." So I sat back down.

By this point the whole audience is screaming. I heard someone yell, "Kill! Kill!" They wanted blood and they were getting it. The bartender had jumped down off the stage and was pounding his fists into the little homeless dude's face like jackhammers as him and Bucky were dragging the guy out. By this point the dude's face looks like raw hamburger and he was just fauceting blood. It was spraying out so much that drops and smears of it were getting on the people they passed. Bucky and the bartender hustled the guy toward the door. There was literally a trail of blood leading from him to the stage. And even in this devastated condition he still kept whimpering, "I want my five minutes!" as he tried to keep swinging at Bucky and the bartender.

Meanwhile, in the audience was this one poet who goes by the name Hal Satan. He's like the token asshole of the poetry scene. Everywhere Hal goes, he's always causing disruptions or getting into fights. Hal's been kicked out of dozens of poetry readings around town. His whole shtick is to be an irritation to anyone and everybody.

Well, in the middle of the bedlam, Hal Satan jumps up on stage, picks up the homeless guy's beat-up old acoustic guitar, starts swinging it around his head, and then Wham! slams it down onto the stage, smashing it into a thousand pieces. We're talking a total Pete Townsend maneuver, there's hardly anything left of it but wood chips. And I felt really bad about that. Because you knew it was the homeless guy's most prized possession. Here was a dude who didn't have nothing and now along comes Hal Satan and destroys the one thing he had to his name. Besides that, the hippie was still in the process of being beaten to a pulp. It was like how many more indignities could this poor little guy suffer?

Hal Satan was really proud of what he had done. He had the broken neck of the guitar with a few strings dangling off it clutched in his hand and he stood up there on stage, shaking it over his head, screaming, "Hal Satan did this! Hal Satan did this! I take full responsibility for this action!" He kept strutting around the stage like he was on some sadistic macho ego trip.

Hal Satan is screaming on the stage, everyone in the bar is standing up screaming at him, the whole scene was one of utter chaos. It was like the bar was so filled with anger that the air had turned to gasoline fumes and you could have just lit a match and the whole place would have exploded.

By this point, Bucky and the bartender had finally managed to drag the little homeless guy outside. Someone must have called the cops because I could see the red lights flashing in through the front door. Hal Satan was still parading around the stage like a puffed up bantam rooster, but as soon as he saw those cop lights, he shut right up, put his arms down at his sides and quietly and inconspicuously walked out of the club through the side exit. The mighty Hal Satan, instantly humbled by the first sight of the law.

Well, two big fat porker cops come waddling in. And just by the look on their faces, I could tell they thought they'd wandered into a subdivision of Hell. It's about a hundred degrees inside this club and everyone is screaming in fury. The cops must have been afraid they'd wandered into a riot. I could tell they were squeamish that all the anger of the crowd would be focused on them.

"Okay, who saw what went on here?" one of the cops yelled.

"I DID!" screamed a hundred voices at once.

"I'll be a witness," someone volunteered.

"No, me! I saw everything," someone else shouted.

"No, me! I'll make a statement!" People seemed ready to fight over who would be the official witness. Like they'd punch each other out to give the police report. The whole crowd volunteered at once. You could certainly get a lot of statements in a room full of writers. The cops didn't know who to pick.

My girlfriend, Susan, and her friend, Sarah, stood up and said, "We'll be witnesses! We were right up front and had a clear view of the whole thing!"

I whispered in my girlfriend's ear, "Will you please be quiet and sit down. I don't want you to get involved with this."

But she completely ignored me and kept yelling to the cops a few feet away. Now, you know what a freak show the Chameleon is most Monday nights, it's a cross between a zoo and an insane asylum. There are people there with tattooed faces, psychedelic dreadlocks, rings hanging from their eyelids. The cops didn't want to pick one of those Halloween lunatics to give the statement. But then there's my girlfriend and her friend standing here, and they're dressed in casual jeans and sensible sweaters. Looked like a couple of college girls from the suburbs slumming it for the night. Besides that, they're cute. So of course the cops want to take the statement from them. They start escorting the two girls outside to the squad car.

"What's going to happen?" I asked one of the officers.

The cop just looked at me and smiled this evil smile. "Son," he said, "when we get a call to come down to the Chameleon, somebody's going to get arrested."

And you know what the kicker was? After the little homeless guy, I was the next person signed up on the list to read. And the whole time this was happening I was like, 'Man, how am I going to top this?' I was really sweating it. After that, anything would be a letdown. But luckily, I was saved by Bucky who wandered in around that time. He went up to the microphone and said, "Look, everybody, that's about enough excitement for one night. That's the end of the reading. Everyone else signed up on the list can come back and read next week."

I was so relieved. Saved by the bell. But that's not the end. You know what the night's finale was? It happened outside the club.

Once the dude was out the front door, the bartender hustled him over to the street and laid him down on the sidewalk with his head hanging over the curb and his arms pinned behind his back. The little guy is looking facedown into the gutter and blood is flowing like a waterfall out of his nose and mouth. It makes a little stream that goes down the nearest drain. And even as the cops are handcuffing his wrists together, he keeps moaning through his broken teeth, "I want my five minutes. I want my five minutes."

The Rider

"I thought something was a little fishy when he said he needed to get to California to go to parapsychology school," said Sam. "He wanted to become a professional psychic, but that guy couldn't even read his own mind. He had to keep consulting his crystals to figure out his next move."

Sam described him as "the ride from hell," or "the devil in my backseat."

"How did you hook up with this guy?" Dave asked.

"It happened back in the '80s," Sam said. "I was going to Oberlin College in Ohio, and when school let out in June I planned to drive out to California and spend the summer working in a Greenpeace office in San Francisco. I put a notice up on the school ride board to see if I could get extra passengers to help with the driving and gas.

"I ended up with three riders. The other two I can hardly remember. They just blended into the backseat and hardly said a word. As the journey continued I think they said even less because after the first hundred miles on the road we were all terrified of this guy, Igor. I never even found out if that was his real name, but that's what he wanted us to call him. I'm tellin' ya, ride boards can be as dangerous as anonymous sex. Up till that point I'd always thought of them as kind of a cool social networking tool but afterwards they seemed more like a game of Russian roulette.

"Things were weird right from the start. To begin with, Igor's only luggage was a large stack of children's books. Doctor Seuss, Cat In The Hat, Curious George, stuff like that. Oh yeah, and he had a bag of crystals. Igor consulted the crystals every few miles."

"What do you mean?" Dave asked.

"Well, he'd set the crystals on his lap or in front of him. Do these little incantations and hand gestures and I guess the crystals talked to him or something. It's not like anyone else in the car heard them or anything.

"At first I just wrote him off as a harmless hippie. There were lots of those types hanging around Oberlin and I had some experience when it came to acid casualties. But after about an hour on the road, I realized Igor was a little more severe. To begin with, he was manic. Talked like a white streak and you often couldn't get a word in edgewise. And his monologues kept looping way out into the stratosphere. At first I thought Igor was tripping, but when I looked at him in the rearview mirror his pupils weren't dilated and he didn't have those telltale signs of chemical jitteriness which go hand in hand with LSD. His story came out in fragmentary pieces, like a Burroughs cut-up novel, but it soon added up that Igor was so schizophrenic that everyday life for him was like tripping on acid all of the time.

"His appearance set me off, too. A long shaggy beard, wild, unkempt, almost dreadlocked hair. But like I said, people like that weren't uncommon around Oberlin, I was a Deadhead at the time, into the live-and-let-live ethic, and I thought he was just another earth pig in need of a bath. It turned out that Igor was in even greater need of hygiene than we had imagined because around Indiana he confided to us that he had been homeless for the previous year. 'In fact, this car ceiling is the first roof I've had over my head in the past three months,' he said triumphantly. Igor followed this revelation up by telling us that before he was homeless he'd spent a year in a mental institution. I don't think the other passengers said a word for the next three hundred miles. They were a mousey pair, honor students I think, who couldn't accept what was happening to their reality. But I kept talking to Igor. As long as he was talking I could keep track of where his mind was going. It was his silence that I was much more afraid of. Especially with me in the driver's seat and him sitting right behind me.

"So what's in California, Igor?" I asked him at one point.

"I'm going to the Berkeley School of Parapsychology," he replied. "Gonna train to be a psychic."

"And what makes you think you'd be a good psychic?" I asked.

" 'Well, I already hear voices," Igor said. "All the time. I hear them speaking even when no one else does. Sometimes there's so many of them and they're so loud I can't even hear my own voice in my head. That's when I use the crystals to help clear my mind. They're the only voices that matter. But after awhile I realized these voices were other people's thoughts, that I could hear them. But I couldn't always understand what they said, lots of the time it was all garbled. It takes practice to be a good mind reader. That's why I'm going out to California, to train my talent into something I can make a living with.'

"Igor went on to describe the curriculum and the campus at the Berkeley School of Parapsychology. It sounded like he was reciting it straight from some pamphlet he had read somewhere. But in the course of his description it eventually came out that he had never even applied to the college. In fact, he had had no contact with the school at all, didn't have even the most basic entrance forms or any records of his previous schooling. Guess he just planned to get out there and wing it. The illusory nature of his goal became even more apparent when he admitted that the current semester had already been in session for over six weeks. Oh my God, I thought, this whole psychic college thing is just his version of the Holy Grail.

"By this point I had already ascertained that Igor had no money. Not a cent. Nothing to contribute to gas or food. In fact, our middle class liberal human compassion would force me and the other passengers to pay for his basic needs. We'd already bought him a burger at a truck stop. He was heading straight for the streets in Berkeley. This poor deluded soul, I thought. Everywhere he goes he's going to be homeless. There's no dream waiting at the end of the road. But in the meantime, Igor was nothing but dead weight for the trip. And that weight was about to become heavier."

"If you don't have any money or anyone to stay with in California, you're going to be in big trouble when you get out there, Igor. I mean, why don't you go back and stay with your parents in Cleveland for awhile?" I suggested to him somewhere around Illinois. "Let them put you up for awhile so you can save up some money and come back and do California in style."

"I just came from my parent's house," Igor replied cryptically.

"Uh, what happened? Did they kick you out or something?" I asked, afraid of what Igor's real answer might be.

"They weren't there," he replied. "You see, I broke into their house. Burglarized it. And did a pretty messy job of it too. Left clues and fingerprints everywhere and I'm sure they have my fingers on record cause I've had run-ins with the authorities on many occasions. In fact I'm sure they're looking from me right now. Probably have an APB out on me. Guess that means I'm on the run. A fugitive from justice. But it's their justice, not mine."

"Oh great, I thought. Things go from bad to worse. But then I thought of a possible silver lining.

"You didn't happen to take any money when you robbed your parents house, did you?" I asked.

"Nope," Igor replied smugly. "I'm not interested in such worldly things. All I took was my children's books. The books I read when I was little. They don't belong to them anyway. I was tired of seeing them hold my childhood hostage."

"As the miles went by it became quite apparent that the guilt of breaking into his parents' house was weighing heavily on Igor. He kept consulting his crystals for ways to relieve it. Eventually the rocks came up with an answer. Whenever Igor crossed a state border he would have to get out of the car and tear up two of his childhood books. This would slowly release the 'karmatic pus that had built up in his aura.' He did this in a methodical, almost ritualistic way. He would tear out the pages ten at a time and then proceed to tear them up into increasingly smaller squares. Always squares, never circles or irregular shapes. When he had the pages down to the size of confetti he would scatter them away on the breeze. The denuded covers were then burned. It made a hell of a mess. I was always afraid Igor's purification ceremonies would get us arrested for littering. That would have been a blessing in disguise because at least it would have taken this crazy person off our hands. But there were no incidents. Whenever we crossed a state line, I would stop the car and Igor would get out and dispose of another piece of his childhood. The other passengers would stare at him from the backseat in abject horror. I was always tempted to just drive away and leave Igor there. But I never did. I don't know why either. Maybe I just felt sorry for the guy. By the time the trip ended, every one of Igor's childhood books had been destroyed. All of his baggage was gone, it had been strewn over almost a dozen states.

"Now, by this point, I was getting fed up. I'd only kept from acting because I was afraid Igor might be dangerous. But he was shaping up to be a harmless crazy. Another lost soul. Only I was tired of having his smelly, nerve-racking presence in my car. Since we had just entered Colorado I was trying to convince Igor that they probably had much better parapsychology schools in Boulder than in Berkeley. Probably had better homeless shelters, too, but I didn't mention that. I told him Allen Ginsberg, half the Buddhist monks, and two-thirds of the New Age crazies in the country called Boulder home so it had to be a spiritual power zone. Besides, the tuition was probably cheaper in Boulder. But Igor remained firm in his choice of alma maters. Colorado did nothing for his 'sixth sense.' But I kept hard-selling the place. I knew if I planted him there he'd never make it over the Rockies to visit me in San Fran.

" 'Sorry, man,' Igor finally said. 'But there's no ocean here. Most of our consciousness resides in the sea. Over ninety-eight percent of the life force emanates from the tides and the Pacific is right next to Berkeley.'

"What the hell, I couldn't argue with that. So with a heavy heart, I drove straight on through Colorado into Utah. Igor's basic animal needs for food had used up most of the excess cash I had with me. I was afraid we wouldn't have enough gas money to make it to San Francisco. I thought the other passengers were holding out on me, but there was no way to be certain. Those two were completely useless. They looked like brainy types but neither of them ever opened their mouth long enough for me to ascertain whether there was any knowledge floating around behind those shifty eyes.

"One was a boy, the other a girl. She had spent the entire trip in a monotonous mood of suspicious terror. I knew little more than her name, and since she radiated no personality and said nothing, I had even forgotten that somewhere around Kansas. The boy was so similar he could have been her twin except that his hair was darker and his nose more crooked. His only distinguishing characteristic was that he would petulantly whine about having to use the bathroom every twenty-five miles. Both of them wore glasses and weighed about ninety-five pounds each so they'd be no good in a fight if Igor got violent. The two of them treated small talk as if it were streptococcus. Igor may have been crazy, but at least he was good enough at the fine art of conversation to keep me awake on those long night drives. Those two, on the other hand, just sat in the backseat with all the animation of a couple of mildew stains on the upholstery and let me deal with everything. To make matters worse, neither of them could drive."

"You're kidding," Dave said, flabbergasted.

"Nope," Sam replied. "Neither one of them had a driver's license. They just never learned. Guess they were used to having Mommy and Daddy drive them around all the time."

"So you were the only one driving? All the way across the country?" Dave asked.

"Pretty much," Sam sighed.

"That must have been completely exhausting," Dave said. "Even if Igor hadn't been there to make things worse."

"It was pretty bad," Sam said. "In fact, I think I got so tired it began to affect my judgement. You see, Igor could drive. He even still had his license. He kept bugging me to let him drive for awhile. I guess he felt it was the only way he could pull his own weight. Of course I wouldn't let him near the wheel. I didn't even like having him in the front seat. But by the time we hit Nevada I was a zombie, a trembling red-eyed shambles. I was ready to let anyone, I didn't care if it was Francis the Talking Mule, take over for me. What the hell, I figured, the roads are straight and flat. So I let Igor drive."

"You didn't!" Dave exclaimed.

"I did," Sam replied with quiet embarrassment.

"What happened? I'm surprised you're here to tell the tale."

"Well, he got behind the wheel and I rode shotgun," Sam said. "We took off down the road. Going twenty-five miles per hour. Cars were whizzing past us honking and giving us the finger. I thought we were sure to be the head car in a huge pileup. No matter what I said to him, Igor wouldn't drive any faster. He insisted it wouldn't be safe. Even when the car idled up to thirty on a downhill, he'd jam on the brakes to slow it down. But I didn't make him stop driving because I was just too tired.

"Then I began to notice something. He was having real problems with the road signs at exits. Kept missing them. He'd ask how far it was to the next town when we'd just passed a mileage marker. Finally I was like, 'Hey, Igor, what's the problem? Can't you read? Are you illiterate?' 'No,' he replied lightheartedly. 'I wear glasses. But I lost them over a year ago.' I asked him if I could see his driver's license. He sheepishly handed it over. According to that he was legally blind."

"Maybe Igor should have consulted the crystals to tell him how to steer the road," Dave suggested.

"Maybe he should have held the crystals over his eyes and used them as a set of glasses," Sam replied acidly.

"Did you let him drive any more?" Dave asked.

"Only for another fifty to a hundred miles." Sam shrugged his shoulders. "What can I say? By that point I'd lost all my reason. We eventually made it to San Francisco unharmed."

"Whatever happened to Igor?" Dave asked. "Did you ever see him again? Or did he just disappear into the ranks of the homeless?"

"Actually," Sam said, "Igor became a famous guru and spiritual healer. Was the head of one of the biggest cults in the country with thousands of followers nationwide. Eventually he expanded into TV ministries and Dial-A-Psychic phone lines. Igor had all these yuppies writing him checks, signing over their life savings and estates to him. Just raking it in hand over fist. Regardless of his eyesight, the metaphysical press touted Igor as 'the greatest visionary of the twentieth century.' He wrote some self-help book on escaping your childhood that sold over ten million copies worldwide. Now he owns two mansions in the Berkeley Hills and I've heard he even plans on building a huge shrine in Boulder, Colorado."

"I guess those crystals steered him pretty well," Dave said.

FLASHBACKS and PREMONITIONS

ONE

It was a gray overcast day trembling on the edge of rain. End of March with winter squeezing out its last polar moans. Garbage and paper cups blew across my backyard to be caught in the skeletal garden. I had that sour used-up feeling you get from drinking yourself to sleep. Wake up feeling more exhausted than when you went to bed. And I had had that dream again. Lately I've been plagued by a recurring nightmare of an odd creature trapped in a fibrous womb. The thing is vaguely humanoid with a snarling demonic face, only it has no skin. All its viscera, bone gristle, and nerve tissues are open to the air. The inside of the womb is lined with long fibers writhing like hyperactive ganglia. These fibers bore into the creature like roots whenever it is still, causing great pain. So the creature must be in constant motion, thrashing about tearing them out and as a result, it never sleeps.

A chill drizzle starts, the type that drips down into the shadowed areas of your thoughts, the cold places you don't want to be touched. A biker friend told me today that one of my ex-girlfriends is selling herself at the truck-stop. I think of her child's body shivering in the end of winter rain, in the company of harsh men who haven't washed their hands in fifteen years, escaping venereal infections by a penis's width.

I'm still paying for my last girlfriend. After two years of living together in bliss, I just couldn't take anymore. One Friday morning I went up to her and said, "Look. It's over. I can't stand this relationship any longer. It's been dead for me for months only I just didn't have the nerve to tell you. But you've pushed me too far. I want you out. I'm going away for the weekend. When I come back on Sunday night I want all your stuff and you moved out." And I left.

I expected her to break everything I owned, but when I returned late Sunday the apartment was immaculate. She had cleaned the place top to bottom. All her things were gone. None of my belongings were smashed, missing, or burned. She even did the dishes. The only thing out of place in the entire apartment was the phone off the hook. I hung it up. At the end of the month my phone bill knocked me to a twitch. It turns out that as soon as I left on Friday afternoon she called an answering service in Hong Kong, and left the phone off the hook. It had been off the hook all weekend. My phone bill was $5,200.

I read today about a scientist who has discovered that what we call "love" is really an addiction to glandular chemicals secreted by the skin of our loved one. These chemicals are transferred through kissing and sex and this is why the mouth has become such a formidable erotic object. This explains a lot of things. It explains why you hurt physically as well as mentally after a breakup, even when you were the one who initiated the split. It explains a lot about obsession. Madness accompanies any form of drug withdrawal.

I broke up with another girlfriend a few years ago. I had seventeen pairs of shoes and she stole all the right-foot ones. As she drove back to her parents' home in New England she threw a shoe out the window every few miles along the turnpike. I can see her now: "Oh, mile post 57, time to throw out a Nike." I don't know what it is about my personality that brings such violent reprisals from women. Sometimes I feel it is their limitless invention in revenge which makes me love them so desperately.

Gray wind blows right through me. Rain rings in evening puddles. My roommate didn't work today. So as soon as he got up he plopped into an easy chair and began sucking on a clay pipe of opiated hashish till his eyes were lazy glass beads rolling about in a head full of syrup. He watched the cable news for twelve hours. Endless disasters and ugly diplomats parading through the reflections on his erased eyes, his skin clammy as a manta ray's belly in the blue video glow. Yesterday he broke up with a girl whose name he can't remember.

The comic book freak just walked into my store and started talking to me. He looked like a redneck, blue jeans, Spiderman t-shirt and a baseball cap that said "Visitor" on the visor. A fuzzy Saint Bernard beard was punctured by the pink ring of his lips. He knew his stuff about both Marvel and DC. For a while we discussed the sociological implications of Iron Man's costume change, Thor growing a beard, and Captain America's retirement. I knew we were headed for trouble when he began to talk about his philosophy of life.

"Now, you have the big bang," he said, "and scientists tell us that when the universe started it was only as big as the head of a pin and then Bam! and you have this huge mass of complex energy moving outwards. Some of that energy forms into matter, like buildings, trees, and you and me but the rest of it is still moving outward. And what is going to give that energy form? The laws of physics. Basically other forms of energy will mold it. Now, you have all these comic book writers putting out all these comics. They're just providing the grid or the structure. But all the people who read them are fleshing out all the details of these stories with their own imaginations. So that in the end you have a completely realized universe. And all this mental energy flows out from the comic book writers and readers, and shapes that leftover energy from the big bang into a new dimension that exists just beyond the barriers of our five senses. Now, let's go back to where the universe was the size of a pinhead. After the explosion when everything is moving outwards, what's left where that pinhead was? A black hole. Everything that's moving outwards obeys the laws of physics, but in the black hole is the negative side of the universe, and that's where the doors open and all possibilities exist simultaneously."

Not another one of these freaks, I thought. Time to play devil's advocate.

"Yes," I said, "but once the laws of physics reach their logical conclusion, won't the big bang change direction and everything will begin to contract?"

"That's right," he said. "Time will go backwards and all things will move towards order instead of entropy. Broken dishes will fall back onto tables whole. Mothers will bitch at their kids not to unchew so fast or they won't get indigestion."

"People will learn to hate order as much as we hate chaos," I said. "The turds will be flying out of the toilets up everyone's asses. God, what a horrible place to live!"

"Hey, you want to hear a poem?" I asked.

"Okay," she said.

"Okay, this one is called 'This Is About Sexual Intercourse'. It's the early worm who gets the bird / in the bush / but a worm in the bush / is worth two in the hand."

"That poem sucks."

"Hey, one day those words will be written on the walls of subway stations across America. And Europe, too. Little bald skinheads will be my disciples and I shall speak to them in the language of the killer bees."

"What's it sound like?"

"Bzzz. Bzzz. Very simple language. Only has one word."

"Would you stop writing? I want to go to sleep. What's this, your third novel? Are you going to type it, too? Come on! I want to go to sleep. Stop writing. Stop writing! Stop..."

"Start? Did you say start over? Okay. Hey, you want to hear a poem?"

"Okay."

"Okay, this one is called...

"Stop..."

"Start? Did you say start over? Okay..."

Finally, she said, "Hey, I think this novel has a skip in it."

Last night me and my girlfriend came home from the movies, turned on the kitchen light and the linoleum floor was covered with roaches. Both of us shrieked and ran about crushing them into little circles of mush.

The apartment has no screens and so our bedroom is full of insects and little clusters of legs crawl across us in our sleep. In the living room, a singing of crickets. Moths are everywhere, flickering specks on light bulbs. I find that when you crush them they are such dry little creatures. A pile of powder is all that's left between your fingers. My girlfriend told me her grandmother believed that moth powder had healing powers so every day she used to grind little wings into her cup of coffee.

Last night my girlfriend had a nightmare that our apartment was infested with two-foot long roaches. After we had killed them with baseball bats and poison we used the leftover shells as casserole dishes.

Thunderstorms are all around but the rain never falls here.

Yeah, I've smoked holes in my lungs and I gotta admit it was just a quick high, but isn't everything that way, even if you've worked ten years on it, the rush only lasts a second, all the long hours of our lives spent in the service of these tiny fragments of time, because they're the only places we ever owned something, and even though it always got away, and always too quickly, at least for a second, we had it. And that's where we breathe.

God, we thought we were artists! Slaving away in our ivory towers, searching for the hidden formula, the great unknown theory that would really change everything, the ultimate painting, the definitive song, but we were really just smoking, drinking, and fucking ourselves to death, just like everyone else.

My girlfriend is gone for two months and everything seems empty. The apartment is a soup of compressed time. I don't live time there, it merely flows through the place slowly like a numbing syrup. At least the insects seem excited. I run my fingers over the moldering woodwork in search of some form of chronology. What if the dozens of layers of paint on the walls are a stratigraphy filled with the layered fossils of past residents?

My insomnia is returning and I drift about the rooms like a ghost, late at night clinging to a fragile lightbulb, fighting the moths for space. Maybe this is a process of emptying out. Summer is good for that. To me it is always a time of dying inside. Dying in the middle of all that green life. When sleep comes it is just patches of nightmares. We still have no screens in the apartment and in the night insects with dozens of elbows crawl into my hair and suck the sweat from my scalp. Cellophane wings rasp in the dark corners and roaches twitch beneath the refrigerator. A plague of insects has fallen on this town and every time you walk out your back door you step on dozens of them.

There is a big machine which rides up and down the railroad tracks behind the apartment and eats things. It sits on its own wheeled platform with rows of whirling fang-like knives that chew up the underbrush. There is a lower set of rending mandibles set at ground level. These tear up the steel tracks and railroad ties. When small animals like rabbits and dogs get caught by it they are instantly reduced to blobs of hamburger dotting its wake of shredded branches and splintered ties. I understand it is there to clear the tracks, but it seems very frightening that no one runs it. It must be controlled by a computer at the railroad company. Or maybe it's just a rogue machine, a shark on the tracks, avoiding the predatory freight trains and scavenging for what it can get.

I saw a show on TV the other night done by the Christian Broadcasting Network. It attempted to explain the devil in scientific terms. According to their theory, evil is an energy field, a form of dark magnetism. Missionaries are sent into the parts of this world where these fields are strongest in an attempt to disrupt them. Often these missionaries are going to certain death. But their deaths, called martyrdom by the broadcast, up the numbers of new missionary applications by 25 percent. Maybe these missionaries think they're fighting the magnetism but it's really just dragging them to their own destruction.

There is no doubt that love is an attraction. People are drawn together. It's a form of pure light magnetism. But evil also has its pull.

Went to the Deerpark Tavern last night and tied on an ugly drunk buzz. Phillip loaned me his mug so I got plastered on about two dollars. The Deerpark Tavern is such a haven for drunks. For most local alkies it's a second home. The bar sells special mugs to their regulars which let them drink at a reduced rate. If you're an official mug holder, beers are only two bucks apiece. The only thing is the mugs cost like fifteen dollars and I was always too cheap to buy one. Therefore I had to rely on borrowing my friends' mugs to support my cut-rate version of alcoholism. Another problem with the mugs is that the people who usually buy them are such hardcore alkies that they're always losing them or dropping them as they stumble home. On a good night I always pass a number of shattered mugs on the sidewalk as I walk home after last call.

On my way there I met some guy I used to work with in the kitchen at Klondike Kate's, only tonight he was sitting out front on the restaurant's porch drinking mixed drinks. Turns out he's now the manager of Jiffy Lube and making bookoo bucks. It was nice to hang out with him out front in the luxury zone of Kate's instead of in the sweatshop in back. We both had made it out of that hole. I left and rode down to the Deerpark feeling mighty successful and with the sense that my friends were moving up, too. But walking into the Park was a sobering experience. All my old cronies stuck in the waitress and cook rut were there. All the losers I hadn't seen in months. I just can't deal with the old sop scene, I've forgotten how to wear all the masks. I had forgotten that being drunk is more of an acting job than relaxation and letting loose who you really are.

Oh, classic scene. Some guy is leaning up against the bar just taking in the crowd when this short chick runs up to him and starts rubbing herself all over him. I'm talking full body contact from the knees up, and her tits are drumming out a march on the dude's chest. Then she starts making all these lewd suggestions about what they're going to do back at her place and the guy's just taking it all in stride, like he expects it and isn't surprised, so I figure it's his girlfriend and he looks down and lets out the corker, "Well, are you going to introduce yourself?" Classic.

Then there's this one outrageous blond in the main room with five guys sitting at her table hitting on her and all the guys are blond too and look exactly like her. I have a little theory about how people only sleep with people who look like them. Well, that idea gets blown out of the water because at about ten minutes to last call some hunk of a brunette guy sits down at the table and starts laying a smooth rap on her. And she ends up leaving with the brunette! Not only that, but as they're walking out she tucks a five dollar bill into his shirt pocket like it's a tip or something. Smooth operator.

I talked to Susan. She started telling me how she's going to go back to school and get her degree, and she kept talking on and on about her plans and they get more way out until it's just sci-fi, and she claims she'll travel around the world every year and learn different languages but she hasn't left Newark in five years, never will, can't even hold down a minimum wage job, or any job, and has to live at home half the time because she's such a complete mess.

I rapped with Jackie, Jorge's old girlfriend, and I think she was trying to pick me up because she latched on real tight in that blurry half-hour after last call, but it would have been too weird, although the irony of picking up one of my best friend's girlfriends didn't escape me. But I don't know what I want except for you to come back, and all my signals are scrambled especially in these late night drunks where all I have to do is drink myself into nothing because there is no one in the bed at home, and I think I may have found some secret of humor because I laugh a lot even though I'm depressed most of the time but things are just funny. Humor grows in everything and you just have to see it and even on the days I come really close to offing myself I laugh at least a dozen times.

Now that I have no one to sleep with, no body to adhere and respond to in the dark empty hours, I sleep like a dead man. Flat on my back, arms at the sides, without moving all night. When I get up the next morning there is a wet spot of sweat in the exact shape of my body like a chalk outline on a sidewalk. Sometimes I even think I sleep with my eyes open. Now that you're gone I feel a lot smaller, nothing has the same breadth or scope anymore, things happen, wonderful things, but they just seem trite and unimportant. You are a lot bigger than I thought you were. I miss the tiny little hairs at the base of your back.

I have been sick all week and in Los Angeles they are driving around the highways shooting each other. High speed with a sawed-off shotgun hanging out the driver's side window. They're killing each other over minor traffic disputes such as who cut off who at the exit ramp. Close to the edge survivalists reaching critical mass in the cookers of their cars. This summer the heat and insects are everywhere. Heatwaves dust across the heartland. My dreams are swollen and lumpy with fever. And the congressional hearings never seem to end. I feel as if I am spiraling downwards in search of a bottom, but I just go deeper and deeper.

I have a virus and I can feel those blank faceless bastards hiding in the shadows of my veins. Smooth spherical killing machines hijacking my DNA, killing me with my own body, exploding my cells out from the insides with their mindless duplicates, strumming my pain on their fever strings. And in my brain they slip out from the veins into the wondrous energy of thought and mutate into ideas, a new plague transmitted by mental telepathy.

There are so many vicious new viruses around these days. They rise up from the waste dumps, get cooked up like crack bars in nuclear reactors. When you're that simple almost nothing can kill you. So simple you aren't even really alive. Epilepsy takes all the beautiful multifaceted patterns of thought and shatters them, breaks them down to one step from nothing, a flat wave thought, a moronic monotone hum. And the wondrous human creature with all its beautiful nuances becomes a drooling idiot. Viruses are trying to do this to everything that is alive. They want to take all the exquisite species, and tear them down to their own simple structure. Viruses take you over, use your raw materials to replicate themselves. If the virus equation is allowed to follow through to its end they will replace all living things, and the landscapes of this planet will be covered with what looks like huge piles of b-bs. Inert matter waiting for new prey. Strange how in a world helplessly spiraling into ever increasing complexity, viruses want only to simplify things. And what is more simple than nonexistence?

I look at my arms and they're these wasted white things where the cuts don't heal. Zits and sores are breaking out on my back and I've dropped ten pounds. Ever notice how as soon as one bug makes a hole in your defenses all his bacterial buddies decide to move in too and catch a free ride on the deal? I'm beginning to forget what my girlfriend's voice sounds like and it's still weeks till she'll be back.

Doesn't matter. Right now I'm too sick to enjoy her. The apartment is all full of insects. These goddamn headaches. Funny how the bad things all happen at once.

After seven ages of Hell the planets all lined up, the Mayan calendar ended, and one Sunday morning mankind stepped into a new age of enlightenment. Cultists, witches, and hippies gathered at Stonehenge, Mt. Shasta, Easter Island, and other areas of mystic power to link up consciousness. The time of unity was at hand. Dolphins were committing suicide on North American beaches and mines lurked in the Persian Gulf, but for at least this Sunday morning people turned away from all that, stared into the dawn sun, and held hands. It was called the Harmonic Convergence and even the Christians who hate and disapprove of everything thought it was a good idea. Flower children on the grass in Central Park, flute music echoing off the pyramids. According to the Mayans we were entering thirteen ages of heaven when science and reason will cure all ills. Maybe.

I am no longer sick. My woman is coming home. Sunday night was the first time I didn't have nightmares in as long as I can remember. Just after dawn Rudolf Hess strangled himself and the prison which held the last of the Nazis will be torn down. It takes time to burn down the cities of Hell. Our world is still a wounded machine creaking with problems, in need of oil, but we have turned our vision another way, and finally, hopefully, we are headed in the right direction.

Una is full and ripe, the many rolls of her flesh inviting without hiding terror. She is smooth and round, her great breasts flowing out like two snow slides, as finely sculptured as footballs, but gentle, she has that surrounding comfort, the maternal and bovine tenderness of the Earth Mother. Ruth wishes she had this but she just isn't fat enough. She has a quick conniving sleekness. Pantherlike. Her pert little breasts always alert. Her fingers alive with a history of cunning and sexual caresses to a specific end. With a body taut and sensitive as an electric wire, she has the manipulation and intrigue one only finds in a skinny person. Though less appealing sexually, this makes her far more interesting and desirable.

She was fat and ugly, shaped like a turnip and I made sure I brought her home long after dark, far into the night, and both of us were very drunk. She wore no underwear and there was a huge hole in the crotch of her tattered fishnet stockings and I fucked her through that hole, being unable to solve the geometry of her clothes. Nameless late night numb fumbling. A persistent biological circuit eclipsed by alcohol, fingers in the slurred vision. The next morning we dress in silence and my head is about to explode as I run about the apartment chewing aspirins to powder.

She was a beautiful trusting thing, well padded with luminous white flesh and I had just gotten her top off and was lifting the weight of those delicious round things in the ivy behind the wall somewhere after midnight. I didn't remember how I had gotten here but I liked where I was and the friendly rolls of her flesh drifted beneath my hands when suddenly the lights of a dozen cop cars spiraled along the other side of the wall, sirens and bullhorns were everywhere as they busted a party across the street and I had just succeeded in getting her bottoms off too when about fifty people trying to escape the party jumped over the wall all around us and one guy even crawled up to the two of us and asked if we knew how to get away. In the end we went to her place. It turned out she was living in the front seat of an El Camino parked in the Super Fresh parking lot. For a while we played with each other, dodging the gear shift, too drunk for real lust, and there was not enough room for me between her belly and the dash. Eventually she dropped off to sleep like an overstuffed teddy bear and I walked home smiling through the 4 a.m. chill, licking her wetness from my fingertips.

Vague opium visions, black lungs, distant landscapes green.

Large-breasted woman spinning round like a black widow on a thread, a string of shrunken heads round her neck, plump round woman with white teeth filed down sharp, the smile of a great white shark. And a moist valley between her thighs, the primal hole searching for the missing link that is my dick, wet volcanic valley, hungry clam, orgasmic bivalve steaming a mist that smells of jungle funk, crabs washing up on her shores and an asshole like a dark star, a black hole, that will swallow anything deeper, deeper, oh black hole honey I'm making white.

My woman finally came back home and when she asked me if I had slept around on her I lied and said no. She claims she has been faithful but I know this isn't true. Her vagina isn't tight enough. I want to get angry but I cannot. We are strangers. By the time she returned I had forgotten what she looked like. She no longer loves me. To me she is still everything. But I will not tell her that. Men always love much more than they will admit to. We have much work to do if our love is to return. Our eyes avoid each other's or do not understand the language of long stares. Before she left we would lay around all day naked in the summer heat, but now we are clothed in an awkward modesty. I feel as if my face has once again been rubbed in the excrement of life. I understand that I cannot own anyone. Happiness cannot be worked for, money and power cannot buy it, rich men are as sad as paupers, love brings as much joy as despair and all through the medium of trauma. Happiness only occurs through cosmic accident. I see her wander about these rooms, a new being fresh from a cocoon. Autumn is coming. The insects are dying. I walk through the yard, pick up one of the first fallen leaves and remember how green it was in summer, slick with rain. Now it is a corpse, brown and curled. I crush it to dust in my fingers and feel the wind blow it away.

Chaos came back from the West last night. As always he was just drifting through. Working for two weeks in Milwaukee to make enough money to continue his nomadic wanderings. He had been living in a bike locker in San Francisco. For a while he had lived in a youth hostel and worked as a bicycle messenger but he came to the conclusion that he hated authority and decided to quit and do the homeless route, panhandling for a few dollars a day, eating for free in soup kitchens. The holidays were approaching and he was beginning to feel the homeward tug when a biker friend approached him and asked if he'd be up for a ride back East. Chaos, who had just terminated a particularly sour love affair, said what the hell. They went from San Francisco to the shores of the Atlantic in forty-six hours and forty minutes, a new world record. They only stopped the '67 Ford once in Texas to take a crap and do more speed. Whenever anyone had to take a piss they did it in a beer bottle and threw it out the window, preferably at a hitchhiker. Chaos recounted the trip in a series of broken speed freak glimpses: the way that at sunset in the painted desert the shadows are solid as bones and red rocks jagged as scales; the smell of Louisiana bayous; a purple sky over Albuquerque. But now that he was on the East Coast he couldn't wait to get back to San Francisco. He tried to get me to go back with him but I told him I was afraid of earthquakes.

"That's the thing," he said. "I mean, you talk to these people out there, eighty percent of them are from back East, there's no such thing as a native Californian. But you hang out with these people, and they get a few drinks in them, and they begin to confide in you that the reason they really moved out there is because they want to be at the site of a great natural disaster."

He went on to tell me about another journey he had made. He and a biker friend had driven their motorcycles south from San Francisco. Ostensibly they were headed for L.A. and Malibu but their real destinations were fairly general.

"Our first night on the road we slept in a ditch. God, it was titty bit nipple cold, the next morning when we woke up there was frost all over us, on our pants and leather jackets, even in our hair. We hit the Rainbow Gathering, too. This beautiful valley of redwoods with about ten thousand hippies and Deadheads in it. They're all running around in tie-dyed dresses and rawhide boots, the Krishnas are prancing around in their peach smocks, and then we show up on our choppers dressed from head to toe in black leather and chains, the guy I'm with is two hundred and fifty pounds of beer belly and biceps and he's wearing a spiked Prussian helmet. I mean, we were a presence! While we're there we go by some food camp and this flaky lady serves us spaghetti with psilocybin mushrooms in it. About an hour later I can't tell the tracers from the mosquitoes! Some flower child is running around with a chalice, and she comes up to us and asks if we want a sip of 'the water of life.' I'm like, 'No thanks. I have enough life for one afternoon, thank you.'

"Then we went on down to L.A. I spent the night sleeping in the bed of the girlfriend of the lead singer of the Red Hot Chili Peppers. Unfortunately, I wasn't sleeping with her. While the Chili Peppers were playing a show, she goes out and buys an eightball of coke and five of us sit around and do the whole damn thing. We just keep doing it and doing it and doing it till suddenly the sky's all pink with the sun coming up and there's five fat lines left but nobody can do anymore."

"So... you did them?"

"No, I walked out the front door and threw up. God, I love L.A.!"

Yesterday as I ran out of the house late for work there were two fetal pigs laying on my front doorstep. I do not know how they got there or who would have left them. Later that day Flower dusted in from the West. Last time I saw her she had a mohawk and wore only black. Now dreadlocks snaked round her moon white face and a tie-dyed robe covered her lush body. She was living in a schoolbus on the beach in Santa Cruz and had come back East on a whim. Things had changed. Now she was a Deadhead, followed Jerry, and had given away all her old punk albums. Much of this transformation was due to a guy she had been living with. He was one of those people whose life is a disaster of excess in both the positive and negative scales. Monumental good luck followed by hellish failures. Doomed to extremes. A metronome continually tickling both poles of fortune.

After a dim youth spent in the woods of Wisconsin he felt an inner tug and was drawn to the West on invisible strings. That pull terminated in San Francisco in the Haight Ashbury section of town. It was 1967 and love was everywhere. He discovered marijuana and the music of the soul. His consciousness developed. Hippies grooving on all-night rap sessions in ratty cold water flats. Beautiful women opening themselves like flowers. Flower children like the Flower he would find twenty years later. The Haight was immune to hate, it was a tiny slice of paradise, a magic city in the larger city. And all this was threatened with destruction by the festering sore of Vietnam.

He went to the war twice. Volunteered. You see, he had a plan. He'd enlist, go through boot camp, all the preliminary training, and when they shipped him out and set him on the front lines he'd refuse to fire his gun. Sit there in the trenches and just plain not fight. If everyone did this, it would be a tremendous waste of money, training cost plenty, and after awhile the government wouldn't be able to afford the war.

But after boot camp he didn't go to the jungle. They sent him to northern Alaska instead. Up inside the Arctic Circle. A two-month duty served entirely underground. He was a guard in the nuclear missile silos. Cold concrete hallways and flickering control rooms. He marched with his puny rifle past missiles five stories high pointed at Russia. What was he protecting them from? Two months without seeing the sun or breathing real air. Hallways, endless cold gray concrete hallways. No plants. No animals. No windows. No women. One of the only human things in this environment was a fellow private named José. José was a first generation Mexican American from L.A. Not even boot camp had managed to work off his beer gut. Whenever they had duty together him and José would sneak off into the ventilation ducts and smoke huge spliffs of Panama Red. Then they'd hang around for hours in one of the empty control rooms, staring out the observation windows at the missiles and talking about anything.

The first time he ever did acid was during that two-month duty. Subterranean tripping. José gave him the blotter one day when they had to pull a particularly long guard duty. Usually they were completely alone in the concrete halls. It was rare that they ever saw a superior officer. Soon the cement pulsed and wavered and they ran giggling between the nuclear missiles. He saw how ridiculous this whole thing was. What were they guarding against? It would take a hydrogen bomb to penetrate this underground place. If a Russian missile suddenly came crashing through the ceiling, what were they supposed to do? Shoot at it? Him and José were sitting in one of the empty control rooms, the computer banks murmuring all around them. Outside the observation window the missiles loomed like huge phallic symbols. He had his feet up on a desk. José had rolled a joint the size of a cigar and they were passing it back and forth between them. José was giggling as he shut down the fail safe commands and armed one of the warheads. All systems go. The missile was ready to be launched.

"It's so easy," said José as he pulled the protective covering off an ominous red button. This was the final command, if pressed, it would launch the warhead. "Hey man, look at this," said José. "Just think." And he jabbed at the red button with the huge smoldering roach.

The next day he went to the C.O. and told him he was not fit for military service. He explained why he was a hippie, why he smoked pot, why he didn't want to kill anyone. All he wanted to do was make love. For three hours he told the C.O. everything. The Major just sat there stone-faced, listening the whole time. After he had said his piece, the Major sighed and said, "Well, son, I think we're going to have to get you out of the army. I'm going to arrange for you to be transferred to a new position that'll get you out of the army in six months."

The new assignment was on the frontline in Cambodia. His plan had not changed. But he didn't even get a chance to not fire his gun. As his platoon was being airlifted into their first combat position, the helicopter was hit by a mortar and went spinning down through the palms. The crash killed five men and his femur was so badly shattered that he had to be shipped stateside for surgery. He received an honorable discharge and a Purple Heart. All his superior officers congratulated him on what a brave soldier he was.

He returned to the Haight to regain his sense of focus. After two years of love, acid, and experience he had nursed his bum leg back to the point where he could reenlist. This time they sent him straight to the jungle. On his second first combat mission, in the heat of battle, he refused to fire his gun. The Sergeant flew into a rage and tried to shoot him. He had to knock the Sergeant out with his gun butt.

They court-martialed him and he spent a year in the brig before being given a dishonorable discharge. He valued this much more than the Purple Heart. Years of grand experiences went by. The war ended and the '60s cooled. Most of the hippies faded away. He bounced around the country, unable to stick to anything. Then in the summer of '85 he met Flower at a Grateful Dead concert. They had an immediate magnetic attraction. For a while she was his focus, and they traveled around in her schoolbus, following the Dead, selling tie-dyes, and tripping their brains out.

A few years passed and things began to turn dark. It was right before the Harmonic Convergence and all the bad karma was welling up in a tidal wave. Fifteen hundred people at the Rainbow Gathering had come down with a rare form of dysentery. Many of their friends had died and crossed over that summer. Evil was in the air. And then Flower started freaking. They were at a Dead show. Which one? Neither of them can remember. Flower was having the worst period of her life. She had to change her tampon every fifteen minutes and still the blood just gushed down her legs. It was sticky hot, 100 degrees all day and at night it never dropped below 90. They were buying acid from some Dylan clone in the parking lot of the Coliseum when Flower just snapped.

She started screaming at the top of her lungs and ran off into the woods at the edge of the parking lot. He looked for hours but could not find her. She was running through the underbrush on all fours, snarling like an animal, blood covering her thighs. The music rippling out of the Coliseum seemed completely evil to her. After the show they found each other in the desolate garbage strewn parking lot. Flower was still lost. She didn't recognize him. He was out of his depth. He needed to get her to help. They got on a plane and flew back East. During the flight she kept telling him that all the passengers were pterodactyls. Flower did not know who this stranger was but she was glad he was helping her. After they got off the plane he handed her over to two other strangers. She did not trust these people but they were very nice and took good care of her. It was not until a couple of months later that she realized the two strangers were her parents. By then he was gone, vanished into the West without leaving an address. Not once, during the entire relationship, did she ever find out what his name was.

Flower told me about her parents. They were made for each other. Thirty years of marital bliss. The perfect couple. That's why Flower hated them. It was like a slap in the face.

They had been childhood sweethearts. Probably played doctor together. Their first dim probings of sexuality fondled out in the fort they had built in the woods behind Farmer Corn's field. Mother said they used to always play house in that fort. Both had the same build. Tall, skinny, with blond hair. Husband less than two inches taller than wife. 69 a perfect fit. Opposites don't attract. The sounds they made in the bedroom above hers often woke Flower late at night. Joyous grateful sounds. Sounds which drove Flower further into the darkness of the room beneath theirs.

They raised three kids and pushed them all through college. College wasn't a choice in that family. It was cardinal law, as inescapable as puberty. They were raising yuppies and failure just wasn't an option. Flower hated them but they had made her strong. She was a survivor.

Mom and Dad had spent every day together. Both had let all their old friends drop away. There seemed to be no desire to make new ones. All they wanted was each other. Father moved his business, a watch repair shop, into the house so he could be close to Mother all day long. She called him "The Perfect Fit." They never fought. They agreed on everything. Their opinions were always the same.

People began to worry when they started to wear matching outfits. Mom threw out all her old wardrobe and bought a new one, tailormade and identical to Dad's. He would start a sentence. Mom would finish it. All the accounts were made in joint names. One day Dad told Flower he thought that him and Mom were the same person. Their souls were one. Spiritually and physically they were melding into a single being. Then for their thirtieth wedding anniversary they both got facelifts that made them look exactly alike.

Aunt Clara thought they had gone crazy. Other relatives tried to get them committed. When Father found out about their attempts he flew into a rage. He invited all the relatives to Thanksgiving dinner and there he laid it on the line. "Look," he said, raising his wine glass as if to commence a toast, "with this facelift all we wanted to do was show the world how much we love each other, and to have a real physical symbol of the steadfastness of our marriage bonds."

Flower stared at the twins at the head of the table. They were strangers. The surgeon had not made one look like the other. Adjustments had been made in both their faces, so the end result was a completely new individual. Her parents had discarded their old profiles like used cocoons and erected a Narcissistic idol in their place.

"This way," father continued, "when one of us dies, heaven forbid, a part of us will live on in the other person."

So that was it. Immortality. Get so close to another being that you can live on in it when your own body dies. A short hitchhike into the void. To survive a little longer in flesh. Was it love that drove them or a pure survival instinct? One never knows the answers to these questions. Biology and feeling become so intermixed their boundaries dissolve.

Then Father and Mother stood as one, rose their glasses and spoke, in perfect synchronization, with one voice. "Now, in the presence of those closest to us, we make this toast... To togetherness! To life!"

My girlfriend and I have somehow managed to stay together. It's been a long rocky road and I don't know if it's been for better or worse. The relationship has become a constant struggle, a continual repairing and maintenance of the invisible bonds between us. As soon as one hole is patched up, another opens. Our love may be nothing more than a desperation to preserve the coupling we believe necessary to our lives. Maybe it's just a paralyzing fear of being alone that keeps us going. Our longterm goals and life plans have been contradicted, compromised, restructured, and finally thrown away in an attempt to reconcile them with the goals of the other. Our vision of the future grows smaller and smaller as we attempt to preserve the present.

Now we live only day to day. Talk of even a few months ahead always causes a violent argument which rankles on and on until we finally reconfine ourselves in the here and now. Commitments would have helped but we were always too close to the edge to make them. Yet our relationship has survived teetering on that edge for two years now. This process produces a constant tension whose only pressure valve is sex. Fucking has been one of the strongest cements for holding us together. The bed at least is not a problem. But there are many problems nebulous and shifting that tear at our hearts and make daily life steadily unpleasant like a persistent disease. Our life together has become a continual chaos of arguments and apologies in which we no longer know what we feel or want.

Most of all, in our struggles we lost that quiet and elusive thing known as ourselves. In our efforts to understand the other person we lost our own identities. Neither of us knows who we are anymore, nor why we stay together. We fight quite often, are completely different people with separate likes and ideas going in different directions and yet our bond survives through the agency of some senseless magnetism. We have grown much, learned a great deal about ourselves and love, yet we are more lost than when we started on this path.

The place had started out so good, I mean it looked nice, with sun coming in the windows and new paint but it just began to go down and I mean down, went shabby with peeling walls and scuffed floors. Toward the end, broken plumbing lines leaked from the ceiling and no matter how hard we tried, there were more cobwebs, empty beer cans and general trash. Even when we cleaned it still looked horrible, and inside that collapsing house our lives fell apart, too.

Toward the end our apartment was a pigsty. The worst place was our room, the floor completely covered three feet deep in our broken shabby possessions: clothes, books, magazines, mirrors, and stuffed animals mixed into an indistinguishable muck that had a path six inches wide cutting through the center of it to the only clean place in the room - the bed where we fucked endlessly, sometimes just as an excuse not to clean the place, an island of purity in the sea of chaos that our belongings and life had become, a life raft we clung to like two shipwrecked survivors screwing madly to forget they have nothing left to drink.

I will go for a bike ride and when I get back she will be gone. I'll take a shower and wash myself for a long time, but first I'll have to empty the tub that she has left, slowly it will drain like all the things of her life that drift as bits of glass in my soft inside. I go to wash my face and sour milk spews from the tap. No matter how hard I wipe I cannot get rid of the smell. I hear omens, will have nightmares, cry spasmodically for ten minutes and then jump for joy because I am finally free. I do this, I do that, I, I, I, I, I. All these sentences begin with I. Not we. Not we.

The day my girlfriend left I masturbated thirty-seven times. There was just no stopping.

It had rained for two weeks in a cold June after a time when we really hadn't had a spring. The day she left was sunny and hot. I choked the humiliation and helped her pack through long periods of silence broken only when one of us sat down to moan. It took us twenty-two hours, all night and through the next day, to separate our things. Even when she was gone I couldn't remember how to sleep and paced about the apartment frantically looking for a wall to punch but you can't hit the inside of your own skull. Outside the windows, the underbrush, weeds, and trees were lush, green to the point of being poisonous.

A week later the apartment filled with insects. I was living in a place where the walls shimmered hallucinogenically with roaches, bills were three months overdue, the electricity had been turned off, and psilocybin mushrooms spilled from my shoes. I let the bugs eat everything I owned. Left all my possessions in that apartment to rot. Because it was time to go down. Time to take a long slide through the cold underbelly of the American night.

Last night when I got home from a Thomas Dolby concert I found my toilet coughing turds out onto the floor. Raw sewage had backed up through my plumbing and oozed upwards from the shower and sink drains, the bathtub was half-full of sludge and a fecal lava crawled across the floor. I didn't know if this was just the excrement of my building or all the #2s of Newark funneling into my apartment. There was nothing to be done. The landlord was just an answering machine and his emergency maintenance number told me to fuck off because they were drunk. So I just went to bed. In my sleep I was plagued by nightmares that sometime during the night a tidal wave of shit would burst from my bathroom, wash through the apartment, and drown me.

I'm rehabilitating my past, waking it up, slapping it in the face, forcing it to become my present. Recharting all the old connections, digging up old lovers and if nothing else at least meeting their friends, going to their parties, moving outwards. I'm once again social, a drifter. No longer an anchor of two, I move through late nights and bars, realms of hallucinogens and experience, all just to watch the sun rise and feel reborn.

I went out to Henlopen State Park to do a drawing of these machine-gun towers that look out over an empty beach and the Atlantic. But as soon as I sat down a cloud of insects - sand fleas, biting flies, ladybugs - descended on me and stung me so repeatedly that I soon had to get up and run. Some places just don't want to give up their images.

Piles of dead horseshoe crabs in clouds of flies. Brine stench. The surf is crowded with tube-shaped worms, clams, fragments of crabs, puzzle pieces of shells. This place is finally becoming alive again.

The beach! I think of all the crazy LSD times I've had here drinking and screaming with other roisterers through a night weave of parties into the pink dawn when we sit red-eyed and shot on the deserted boardwalk watching the garbage blow in front of the sleeping storefronts. The sun oozes up from the sea like a big round orb, a soft fruit. We scream, we yell, we moan, we sing, we move to the West for no reason and squeeze music out of broken instruments. Night movers who sleep till late afternoon every day, whose livers dissect a strange geometry of mixed drinks and hallucinogens. We listen to old music and new, dance always, and are the last people who are not afraid to fuck. Our lives can be shrunk down to the size of a backpack, or a shred of paper with the address of a contact in a strange new city. We are not held down by possessions. We move. We grow.

I think of Chaos in the West, who travels with only a change of clothes and a baseball bat. He claims he's never been able to sleep without a concealed weapon under his bed. I will see him soon, for I am finally going West myself. One of the last things my girlfriend said to me before she left was, "Why do you want to go to San Francisco? Everyone's dead there." Yeah, like she has room to talk, putting her nursing degree to work in an AIDS hospice in Manhattan.

I have been sleeping around in the houses of friends. Staying for a couple of weeks or until they throw me out. And everywhere I go, I sleep in basements. Dim dark rooms full of the cold of the earth, low places where I run the possibilities through my brain beginning to boil. For awhile I lived in a soundproof room underground, a studio with white walls and no windows like a womb and if the alarm for some reason didn't go off I'd sleep for fifteen hours.

I always had dreams there that I was deep underwater in a square bathysphere with sharks cruising the dark spaces outside and even the trucks that passed on the road in front of the house sounded like distant children through all that insulation.

Then I lived in another moldy basement in a house with seventeen cats, ten of which were kittens and at night their fuzzy little bodies would crawl over me in my dreams till the smell of cat shit woke me out of a sound sleep.

Those cats continually pissed and shat on everything I owned. And one of the roommates there was a real alcoholic, woke up and started pounding Buds at ten in the morning and sucked on through the day till he passed out around 4 a.m. He didn't want me to live there so everyday he'd come down and piss on my bed while I was at work. So I would collect spiders from the webby corners of the cellar and spread them between his sheets. One night he caught a black widow, which sucked him on the end of his dick and left him just enough time to jerk off, quoting D. H. Lawrence as he sank into the gloom.

We had started drinking early that evening at I don't know where in Philly and continued through the long sour-mouthed night from one dim haunt to another, sucking at a blurred umbilical cord of mixed drinks till around 3 a.m. I found myself alone in a gay bar thinking about the woman I had lost, drinking frantically to make the brain damage complete. There was a male nude dancer prancing on the table in front of me. He looked ridiculous, like Marcia Brady going bald. He was dancing with a huge lollipop and would occasionally stop and suck on it in a seductive way while giving me the eye. After doing this about five or six times I couldn't stand any more. When his back was turned to me I reached up, snatched his panties, and pulled them down around his ankles. His feet got tied up in them and he fell flat on his face. In a rage he got up and threw the lollipop at me. It landed in my hair and stuck. I ripped it out with a few light brown strands still clinging and threw it back at him. It stuck to the hair on his chest. Then they threw me out.

Tears. Ha! If only it was as simple as mere agony. But a breakup has a thousand nuances of malaise. Fibrous layers of pain, membranes of feeling violently torn apart like our intermingled possessions that now lay in shreds about the apartment floor. Spasms of exultation and then despair. She broke up with me. After two days of crying I had one of the best weeks of my life because I was finally free. But then her brother tells me she is a complete mess. When she dumped me I wanted her to be so unhappy and now that she is I feel guilty as hell. I want to go to her, hug her, comfort her, but that is the worst thing for both of us. Tugging and pushing, magnetic poles lubricated with tears. Magnets that no longer know what to attract.

Somehow I make it through the long dead days without losing my fake expression, my plastic countenance of ease. Then I get home, smoke pot until my neurons are cold and stare at a blank wall in an utter desolation of the soul. She is gone. And all my dreams die with her. I am a half-man, what was once a perfect two, now half full of aching emptiness. Half-blank which keeps the other hemisphere in pain. The unmade man. A fragment.

I'm moving to California. I'll probably get there just in time for the big quake. I don't care. I'll take my place among the rest of the liberals and slide into the ocean with a smile on my face. It has been speculated that California was created by the Republicans as a testing ground for liberal movements. Put all the crazies in one place so you can keep track of them. Build a liberal ghetto. Or maybe they sent them out there to get rid of them. Blame it on an act of God. All those conservative senators will kick back and put their feet up on their desks as the state sinks and there goes the biggest concentration of Democrats ever gathered in one place.

I have to get out of here. Everything I see reminds me of her, a paperclip on the floor, a book we both read, even the state of Pennsylvania. I hope that the other side of the country is far enough away that I can begin to forget.

I saw a friend of mine from college who had moved to Manhattan and she looked like cocaine and plastic surgery. I met a friend of mine doing cancer research for a private institute that'll probably brew a new plague. All people going somewhere while I live underground in my soundproof room like a worm in the land of push push push.

It's so hot this summer. One hundred degrees every day. Records broken. Woodlands burned. Drought. It's as if Mother Earth just got exasperated with humans and opened up her atmosphere to let us all get burnt.

Since the day my girlfriend left it has not rained a drop. An entire month of sweltering heat. I walk the arid streets feeling that the entire atmosphere is hot chicken soup, croplands reduced to twisted wires on cracked plaster. There's no way to get comfortable, it's paralyzing, mind-numbing, brain cooked like opium, and everywhere tempers explode. For three weeks it has been over 100 degrees every day and at night it never drops below 90. The whole country cooked, cooked.

She came back one last time, to settle our affairs. She arrived beneath a sky that was bright orange and nebular. Heat lightning flickered like thoughts in the air. We both knew it was over. She was happy and strong, all her psychosomatic illnesses were gone. She said that she thought we had tried so hard in our relationship to make something good that we had let loose something evil by accident. How could love become so destructive that it had destroyed both of us?

Now she lived on impulse. Everything was magic and she made her decisions based on how she felt, what her intuition told her. It was a crazy way to live but it hadn't failed her yet. A female spirit had come to life inside her and she listened to what it said. She moved deep into the woods and was working at a summer camp where she cared for emotionally disturbed children. Through them she grew, spread her wings through their crazy dreams and smiles till she had become so big I wanted to cry. She had so much to give. The possibilities were endless.

As we talked, the sky grew turbid, bruised, and swollen.

Lightning struck a tree across the street and it fell onto a car passing. She had my root in her hands and we were kissing frantically. So good to have sex with someone who knows just what buttons to push after all the clumsy lovers and strange new parts I've been with this dry month. The rain fell in opaque sheets, as trees screamed with creaking trunks. I was on top of her, sweat raining down, and then amid the lightning we both came, she was crying, I was laughing, the world so much bigger than I thought it was and I didn't even have to travel to find that out. Afterwards she asked, "What are you still doing here?"

And she was right. This place is dead for me, its energies spent. My life caved in here and there are no pieces left to pick up. When she left, the rain slowly trickled to a stop and I walked through town and thought the buildings seemed like skeletons, hollow concrete bones where all the meat of past friendships had long since rotted away. All I have here is dryness and drought. In my dreams I hear the West singing.

You have to learn to let things go, your possessions, your loved ones, all the things that hold you down, gravity is not so heavy and you can fly. I realize that my girlfriend was my positive side. Now that she is gone I can feel the demons welling up in me. I must leave now, fly to the West in search of a good place or at least somewhere where I can explode. The past two days I have been in a fever, rushing about settling affairs, cauterizing all the flayed strands of my life. Too excited to sleep, my mind works frantically through the hot nights calculating possibilities, trying to think it all out when I know that I must go purely on what I feel. I have been thinking too long, doing what I should instead of what I want, pushed, prodded by everyone around me till I could not move. But that is over. Now the motion is inside me. And nothing will stop me.

Nothing ever ends, we may draw a line but it still keeps on

growing, sending out vibrations around it like little big bangs, even the dead still live in the loss of relatives, and so my relationship with my girlfriend, though gone, still grows, but only as hurt, our child of sadness, the fullest emptiness I carry in me every day.

There was no getting away from it. The agonies and terrors had become unendurable. Life without her was too painful to be worth living. I'd been holding up so well, really keeping it together, trying to look on the bright side of things no matter how dim it was. But I couldn't avoid the issue anymore. The despair came in sudden spasms and I was standing in the middle of a crowded street when this one hit. I knew this was it. Time to end it then and there.

I went into a delirium and tried to strangle myself with my own hands. In a couple of minutes I realized how ridiculous this was and threw myself through the plateglass window of a hardware store. I landed in a display of nails which stuck into my skin like a new steel fur. For a moment I was stunned but then I stood up, brushed some of the nails off, and realized much to my chagrin that I was not only alive but still conscious. So I ran covered with blood into the traffic-filled street.

Unfortunately, the first car I threw myself in front of managed to swerve out of the way and ran over three people waiting at a busstop. So I was forced to throw myself at the windshield of the next car. My whole body went right through the glass, rather painlessly, and all that stuck out onto the hood was my feet. All I had managed to sustain was a couple more cuts so I pulled myself out and threw my body at another car. It jammed on its brakes and I bounced around on the hood. The driver's eyes were big Os as I got on all fours and repeatedly banged my head against the windshield until it shattered. When this didn't even knock me out I jumped through three more car windshields but only managed to receive superficial cuts and bruises.

The last car was piloted by a Driver's Ed student and I don't think he ever got his license. As I landed in their laps, the instructor yelled, "That's it! I quit! Fuck the Highway Code!"

I crawled out the passenger side door leaving them covered with my blood and in shock. On the street I tried to throw myself under the wheels of passing cars but they all managed to stop in time except for one Toyota that skidded past me and ran over a policeman who was running into the road to save me. By this time I was laughing hysterically and more determined than ever to end it.

A huge ten-ton truck was bearing down on me. I waited until it got too close to possibly stop and threw myself under its wheels. Unfortunately I landed in a tiny declivity of road construction like a miniature trough in the asphalt. The tires rolled right over me, crushing my legs, but not to the point that any bones were broken. All I got was bad bruises. When I stood up stunned and beaten, the traffic was halted by a stoplight. Pedestrians ran out into the street to subdue me. One of the drivers whose windshield I had jumped through had died of a heart attack. Behind me, a swerving car had knocked off a fire hydrant and a huge geyser jetted toward the sky. The entire block was in ruins but I was still alive.

I was like a sleepwalker when they put me into the ambulance but on the way to the hospital I snapped back to my senses. I knocked out the paramedic next to me with a plasma bottle. Then I punched out the window that separates the rear section from the driver's compartment and began to strangle the driver. The ambulance swerved about the crowded interstate, red lights swirling. The driver bit my fingers till I let go. I made another grab for his neck but the paramedic on the passenger side sunk a hypo full of sodium pentothal into my forearm and I don't remember anything else till I woke up in the mental hospital.

They kept me there for two months in a blur of antidepressants and finally my counselor decided I was sane enough to return to the real world. All in all I had made thirteen attempts at suicide in a five-minute period and had failed every one of them. All I got for my efforts were cuts and bruises, not even a broken bone. I only got six stitches. Hell, I almost killed that many people. What is it that keeps saving me and why won't it let me go?

And so it ends. She came back one more time. I sit in a cheap hotel room in who knows where. Gray light slides through the stained Venetian blinds. Outside the broken bathroom window, beyond the poison ivy, a cornfield lays sullen and green. Before me on the bed my girlfriend murmurs in her bottomless sleep. Even in slumber she is still exhausted.

There were many things she never gave me. I never saw the energy of her summers. She spent them away from me at distant camps helping and healing people I will never know. I never got any of the glow she gave only to children. No, reserved for me was the devastation of her winters, like the last anorexic one when she starved herself because I was trying so desperately to feed her. Her hunger, her trials, her worst moments. My rewards to share with her. People only give me their negative because they know I am strong enough to hold it. But I cannot hold it anymore. There is too much weight and I am very very tired.

TWO

It is all behind me now. Her. That polluted Northeast. All the negative energy that people unloaded on me for years. The further West I go, the lighter I feel. Movement feels good. Living in that place had become physical pain. The best view of Delaware I ever had was of it shrinking in my rearview mirror as me and my kid sister hit the road. Since our breakup, my girlfriend has begun to heal. Now I must go and heal myself. The roads are like a smooth balm. The sky gets bluer, the very air is different. I have begun to grow again.

There were so many evil things that held me in that place. Dark magnetisms. The evil had become so entwined with the good that after a while I could not recognize either. It took me three months away from my girlfriend to see her as the purest event in my life. But what had destroyed us was some slow pollution that had grown in us both malignantly, persistently, until we were forced apart. Our daily lives build subtle traps. One day you look up and realize that you have not left a three block area in the past year. You go to work and walk home and go to work again, a steadily shrinking circle that eventually strangles you. To live life in a repeating pattern, a monotonous routine, completely blinds you. You begin to believe the world is small. But it is constantly growing. To live the dead routine makes you utterly helpless. You cannot tell whether or not you enjoy life. Both joy and pain escape you. Evil slips in and takes their place. And you are too numb to even feel it growing on you like a fungus.

We got to the Mississippi at dusk, huge mighty river of Huck Finn and a thousand inlets and side channels that weave around and through each other like a feast of snakes. It murmured beneath the moon, the strongest water in America and our car threaded the rocky road beside it up through the river valley watching the scaly ripples grow. Our Chevy ground up past steep crags of prehistoric rock and suddenly we were on the plains. Rolling hills and corn corn corn through the dull drab state of Minnesota where they were having a monsoon after not raining there all summer. Then we exploded over a ridge and all eyes were filled with the Missouri River, bigger than the Mississippi where we had crossed it, with a girdle of bare tan hills that went on forever. South Dakota was scorched earth and dying cattle. Farms and whole towns wiped out by drought. A tiny dilapidated house was the only human thing in miles and miles of dried grass.

Big, big, big, bigger than big, humongous, stupongous, these grass hills kept going on and on past ranches and endless monster hills of furrows and hardly a human to spot the sight. Hills like the backs of great slumbering beasts, their fur made of dried grass. This is the land where man begins to shrink, not even his mighty cities can blot the horizon. The hills, the hills that swallow all things, have no end and are ruled only by the blue sky.

The great plains. Fields the size of counties. Lonely little homesteads abandoned in the vastness, their gray wood rotting and all the windows gone, prairie dogs run through what was once a living room. All the grass a scorched dark brown. Drought has killed this land. The fields are stumpy little burn victims that bear no fruit. A lone tree in the middle of fifty square miles of grass.

The Badlands are bad. They look like a child's sandcastles only they're the size of mountains. Up close they're made of something resembling cement that never completely hardened. The weird formations crumble when you climb them. Out of nowhere they rise up like the wiggly alien peaks in a '50s sci-fi movie. Millions of years of sediment are piled line by line in each butte. Bright yellows of sulfur, dark reds of rust, greenish sand, purple gravel, the area is like a spectrum turned on end. Who would have thought so much beautiful land would be in a place like South Dakota? And we took it all from the natives who kept it so clean. Very little lives in the Badlands, the winding gullies are dotted with hardy scrub but little else, there is no water there, though the mountains appear to have been carved by meandering creeks millions of years ago. In parts of South Dakota you can drive for two hours and never see a house, just huge hills of burnt grass, the endless plains which in a zone of less than a thousand feet become the alien grades of the badlands which drop the continent suddenly down a couple thousand feet into the drier hills and endless vistas that are the true start of the West. The West of change and possibility, of endless opportunity and mysterious powers left over from native times, the magic West, the gigantic West, the West where all things can occur.

The clouds move, lakes of shadow over the tan hills. Great blobs of shade break apart and scatter, wheat ripples beneath their touch. The grass hills go well beyond the limits of vision, they shrink into dimples on the western haze. In this country, houses can only be alone. All of them look ancient and empty, their wood becomes gray, raw, and chapped, the rough grain a graffiti of termite tracks. A rusted pump sucks water from the dry earth. Here the silences absorb all things, men are reduced to insects, cities can barely smudge the endless hills, there is too much sky for carbon monoxide to tarnish.

A car can drive for hours on the winding snake of a road and the driver will not say a word. The land eats all his ideas, it is what it is, words bounce off it like fleas, it is too big to be chained by mere theory. The car keeps driving and the road never ends.

When we got to western Wyoming, the Rockies loomed upwards monstrous and prehistoric. From a distance they were dusted with haze, surprising since all the grass along the roadside was dead. But once you got close you realized it was smoke not haze. All of Yellowstone was on fire. Forest fires raged over ridges, reducing whole stands of timber to the most basic element, carbon. The park looked like a Japanese watercolor painting. Huge mountains and pointed firs rising from a white void. A thick fog obscured everything. Some gigantic cloud appeared to have settled in the valleys, but it wasn't mist. No, it was its exact opposite. Smoke. Both humans and buffaloes cried and coughed from the stench of charcoal. The smell got in your clothes, luggage, food, it was everywhere. Forests of black timber skeletons on carpets of ash. Anything you touched left a shadow on your hand. The sun was an angry red eye glaring through valleys of cigarette smoke. All the animals choked and choked and moved to clearer fields. When the sun set, the fires replaced its orb with their own orange glows. Whole ridges were eaten up during the night, deer and moose fled terrified through the darkness. By the end of the next day Wyoming was just a smoke spot, a dark blot on the horizon.

Forest fires move like something alive. They selectively burn. Sometimes everything is reduced to ash and other times only the wings of butterflies are singed. The poor creatures are forced to walk the rest of their lives. I have seen woods where just the underbrush goes, and this gives room and time for new trees to grow. Lower branches of sequoia are burned, leaving only black nubs while the upper branches flourish bushy in the sun. Fires are strange amoebas stretching their tendrils into unknowable places. Firefighters dance around them like cilia. Moose wander the charcoal ridges braying for grass. Soon the grizzlies will eat all the meat. Man lives out of balance. His chaos echoes through the world around him. Nature will clean herself.

We were flying between the smoky trees in Yellowstone when a grizzly bear jumped into the road and I jammed on the brakes almost hitting it. It snarled, black fur raised, eight hundred pounds of gristle, bigger and angrier than anything I'd ever want to fuck with. But it just walked on by, into the charred carbon woods. Down the road we saw a herd of buffalo grazing beneath a perfect western sky. They were little fuzzy silhouettes like cutouts from buffalo nickels, walking about the dry grass floor of a valley lit up by long shadows and crimson clouds. We drove on past steaming lakes and hot sulfur ground till the evening sky turned to charcoal and forest fires lit up the night.

In Yellowstone, there's a valley of bleached dead trees and stricken grass where geysers and volcanic vents hiss and spit out poisons like suppurating sores upon the land. Hot sulfur ground, boiling mud, and steaming pools. A thermal lake exhales its own private cloud, at the side of the lake a boiling waterfall empties into a chill mountain stream. Angelfish and Canadian pike live side by side. A polluted post-nuclear landscape drifted by, noxious clouds and all of it done by nature herself. The whole valley is a sickly yellow like jaundice. Every breath you take smells like sour farts so it's no wonder the buffalo avoid the place. There are whole fields of calcites, algae, and sulfur. Some of these places reach temperatures of more than 195 degrees. These spots are quite unstable, not even raccoons can walk out on them. I often wonder what happened to the first white explorers who discovered this place. Did they venture out over those demonic grounds? Imagine falling into the earth and having it burn you.

Squiggly lines of dry riverbeds flow down light brown

mountains. Dry lakebeds. White desert. Salt crystals bright as flowers in poisoned waterholes. Dust storms near Reno. Burnt brown hills in Nevada. A brush fire alongside the road. We came down from the brown hills and skirted a patch of misty water and between two lumps of land there it was, laid out like hors d'oeuvres on a platter. San Francisco. The magical city with its little square buildings and tall pointed towers, pink garages and bright blue houses. People on the street were smiling. I knew I had come to the right place.

THREE

People move through the hallways around me like ants in a sick hive. The street is black and murmuring low as jazz at midnight. Apartments creak. Beyond my plaster ceiling, in that darkness of mortar and wood around me are the lighted cubes of kitchens and living rooms where people sit smoking silently at tables. Higher up they drink beer and remember old stories. Laughter ripples near the roof. And above the alley, in that square I can see of sky, the stars babble like mouths speaking a language of pure light.

I like this place. It's a cool city. The people accept things. The air is clean. Rode all around today on a motorcycle and saw the city's intricate web, rode up to Bernal Heights and sat on a huge grass hill which gave us a big view but it was only half the city. We rode to the Tenderloin and saw the down-and-out people in their sadness and addictions. An entire street was lined with sex.

Well, me and Chaos went down to the Tenderloin to sink into the shadows. Went into what we thought was a gay bar but it turned out to be a hardcore alcoholic dive filled to the brim with lowlifes, dock types, and she-males. A pretty blond in girl's boots and a black dress was playing pool and paused to scratch her prominent Adam's apple after every ball in the hole. Crack dealers sold eightballs of rock out the back door. When you walked into the place every monkey you had started to scream. The tug of cold numb faceless sex would twitch deep down inside you. A place where anything could happen. But you just sat there and drank and heard the old timers talk about goat. You walked down Turk Street and watched a prostitute get hauled away. Drugs were everywhere and it was dark between the gaudy patches of neon. This is when the street people wake up. And you went into some sleazy peeps and put pieces of metal into a machine to watch some ugly chick with tattoos and saggy tits spin around on a circle of carpet while you stood there, a halo of lights around your head, jacking off frantically so you wouldn't spend too much money. But only Chaos hit jism cause some girl snuck into his booth and pulled off his quick nut with her tonsils. He slipped her a fiver and walked out into the pink light smiling.

On the street it was homeboys and acid dealers, one porno store had a door like a cattle gate. And then we walked away from the lights, to where it was really dark, just garbage, black backyards and concrete, an empty sidewalk our footsteps tap tapped down. Ahead of us this six-foot black guy was just striding, walking tall, proud, and cocky in a white suit. We heard sirens back at the bright part of the Tenderloin. Must be an accident. The black guy just keeps walking without weaving to either side, a straight line down the cement squares. The sirens get louder, closer. He isn't interested, doesn't even bother to turn around. The wails get pealing loud and red flashes turn onto the street. He keeps walking, arms out at his sides, tall, cocky, unhurried. Two police vans and a squad car screech up to the curb beside him. Blue guys jump out aiming high-powered weapons steady at him. Five pigs grab the black man and struggle him convulsively into a van. The door slides shut. The cops drive away and the street is silent again. We start running.

There's this guy at our place who has developed a real hangdog expression. He goes out with a girl who lives here whose life has gone on and on while his stopped four years ago - when he started going out with her. He didn't go to college, he worked to support her chic lifestyle, worked a shitty job that'll never go nowhere so she can snort her steady grams of cocaine. She went to school, has a career, made the right contacts. All he has is want and need and she knows she's in control, sometimes she'll playfully beat him with a belt and he takes it like a good boy, doesn't even complain when she constantly quizzes him on anthropology or the conjugation of French verbs, things he'll never understand, she gives him a long tether but not even enough to hang himself by. She has her friends check up on him, knows his affairs before they happen, confronts him when they are only ideas, makes him feel guilty for things that never happened. She pretends to be interested in men she cannot stand. Acts cold when she just wants to be fucked then and there. But now this boy has fallen on hard times moving from friend's place to friend's place in a continual inability to make rent, from job to lower paying job in a downward spiral. He clings to her desperately, while she tightens the whip around his neck and smiles.

There was an aquarium on the refrigerator that was full of plastic dinosaurs and algae. It had been sitting there festering for months and the dead goldfish floating in the scummy water were all covered with moss. The living room was decorated with torn apart copier machines, jagged microchips and shredded duplicator parts hung off the lamps and picture frames. One of the roommates had been a Barbie freak and her room was jam-packed with the plastic model's Mattel accessories. Lifesize posters of Barbie, Ken, and the Barbie Beauty Center covered every inch of her high-ceilinged walls. On the dresser were three giant Barbie heads with extendible, styleable hair. When she finally moved out her floor was littered with plastic curlers. Oh, yeah. There was also a 15-foot tall green man in the front closet. He was made of papier-mâché and holding his arms out like Jesus. Where else but Chaos's apartment?

Around that time, the bike people moved in. They were a bunch of hippies and punks who traveled around from city to city, working as bicycle messengers. They arrived in a minivan with seven bikes strapped to the roof. Suddenly Chaos had twenty people living in his apartment. It was like having your own gang. Life instantly became a continual party and they were either threading bars through the city or loading into the minivan to drop acid in Yosemite. Then they invited some more friends out to California and there were thirty people living in the apartment. When the nightly parties finally ended, the floors were strewn with sleeping bodies. There were always three or four people passed out in Chaos's bed. The rooms were filled with dirty laundry and rubber pterodactyls. Soon there were new people crashing there every night. When the place got that out of hand Chaos knew his job was done and it was time to move on. Time to bring chaos to someplace new.

I feel okay now but I could disappear at any minute. There are many holes in this city that a person can just slip into and never come back.

I got a job selling holograms, how's that for San Francisco employment? There's a woman I work with who moved to the city ten years before. She had visited and wasn't sure she wanted to stay until one day she was walking through Golden Gate Park and saw a huge wedding. Lots of tuxedos and evening gowns, catered food, white bows and ribbons, pots of flowers were set up through the crowd. The bride wore an elegant wedding dress with a five-foot train all trimmed in lace and satin. There were buttercups in her veil. Their vows had just been exchanged, the couple kissed and turned to face the guests. The bride had a mustache. And that's what made her decide to live in San Francisco. For five years she worked at a geriatric psychotic dating service. All applicants had to be over sixty and a manic depressive or schizophrenic. A minimum of two personalities required. She must have placed some real winners. Finally she quit to work a sane job. What is sanity in this place?

I spent my last thirty bucks on heroin. I don't know if what I got was the real thing cause it was a different color than it's supposed to be but about a half-hour or forty-five minutes after I snorted it I got complete nerve death, everything shut off. A magnificent golden glow lit up my being. There was no head trip but my body just felt so good my brain had to go along with it. When every cell in your nervous system is having an orgasm you don't argue. Then the phone rang. I picked it up and said hello very slowly. They hung up. The phone kept ringing but whenever I picked up the receiver they hung up. When I didn't answer they'd let it ring on and on, forty or fifty times, till I finally got so angry I'd snatch it up and scream, "Who the fuck is this!" Click. OOOommm. Dial tone. I was all alone in the apartment. I finally went on the nod around 2 a.m. and sank deep into REM sleep. At 5, the phone rang. It would ring sixty or seventy times. Then they'd hang up. About ten seconds later it'd start ringing again. This went on for a half-hour. Finally I crawled out of bed and answered it. A slimy demonic voice hissed on the other end, "The front window. Stay away from the front window 'less you want a brick in the side oh yo head." Click. Well, after that I went into the kitchen and got the biggest cutting knife I could find. I broke off a table leg big as a baseball bat and gave it a practice swing. And until dawn I prowled around those rooms poking into closets and shadows with the knife held up high. Around 9 a.m. when the streets were crowded again with sunlight, people, and rationality, I finally figured it was safe enough to crash, so I went back to sleep.

Deej told me about some Haight Street acidhead who went up into the Ozark mountains with two friends for no specific amount of time. Maybe they'd come back, maybe they wouldn't. They took fifteen sheets of clowns and flying eyeballs with them. One guy got poison ivy so bad he scratched bone, another got bit by a rattlesnake he mistook for a woman. The head acidhead lasted longer than the rest, crawling through the underbrush after getting used to waking up melting and sleeping in throbs. One day he was climbing a cliff and saw something furry down below him. He jumped on it. It was a grizzly bear.

Chaos is gone. He got on his bike and rode off over the Golden Gate Bridge at midnight. He said San Francisco was a dead city. The seekers have gone somewhere else. He knew every street, had been through six or seven scenes but something still eluded him. Some inner magic was gone. So he rode off in search of it not even knowing what it was but having to obey the impulse. I can understand his personal omens, the things that pushed him away. He had been working doing telephone surveys. But he soon realized he was not gathering information but disseminating political propaganda. You can change people's minds just by the questions you ask them. "Did you know that such and such a candidate was convicted of sodomizing a minor in 1953? Did you know that Mayor So-and-so was in favor of discrimination against blacks until 1965?" The surveys had helped make or break the careers of local politicians for the past four years. And most of the people he questioned weren't even aware their opinions were being changed. When asked their race, seventy percent of the white people surveyed replied, "Catholic."

The surveys took place at sporadic times. Chaos would be called the night before and told to show up at 9 a.m. at a certain address. Usually it was a hotel room or a basement rented for the specific occasion. The next morning he arrived at an empty room with two tables and six phones. The surveys went on from 9 a.m. till 11:30 at night. A week later he would receive a phone call from the organizer. He'd tell Chaos to meet him in a local cafe where he'd slip him an envelope full of cash. Each time the phone surveys took place in a different place and the organizer never told Chaos his name. But after Chaos had worked for him a number of times the organizer began to loosen up at their cafe meetings and told Chaos that he was trying to make dirty money clean. He received large sums from certain unnamed and probably corrupt sources who wanted specific public figures politically assassinated in office. The organizer said he gave the profits from the surveys to the Nuclear Freeze Fund. It was not until months later that Chaos found out that the organizer was lying. The surveys were really run by the San Francisco Police Department as an intelligence gathering tool. If you're not helping the solution, you're part of the problem.

Chaos quit immediately. He knew what kind of tactics the S.F.P.D. used. When he first moved to the city, he had worked for them as a fundraiser. They had sent him into the Mission to supposedly collect for a police-sponsored United Way drive. People in this part of town couldn't afford to give. Many were fresh off the boat immigrants just starting out. But they all gave because they thought Chaos was a cop who'd blow the whistle on their lack of green cards. A lot of them just thought you had to pay the cops extortion money in America, too. Chaos later found out that only two percent of the revenues gathered ever went to the United Way. All the rest went to the organizer and police paychecks. It disgusted him. Even when you try to work for good there are forces that pervert your efforts into shams.

Crack had begun to invade his neighborhood. The homeboys and rock men would hassle the new wavers on the street in front of his apartment. Chaos's landlord wanted him and his roommates evicted so he could raise the rent. But the roommates refused to move out on their cheap lease. So one night the landlord went to the crack dealers who hung out on the corner and gave them two dozen jugs of red wine if they'd promise to throw the empty bottles through the apartment windows. They did. One landed in Chaos's bed. Now, he's good in a fight and has the craziness it takes to kill someone twice his size. So he ran out the front door, screaming at the top of his lungs, straight at the dealers. But one of the homeboys looked in Chaos's eyes and saw he didn't have what it took. The dealer smiled, then began to laugh at him. Chaos saw the street tilt upwards like a hill and felt his momentum drain away. He had lost something. He stopped in the middle of the street and walked sheepishly away, the crack dealers laughing behind his back. He didn't know where he had lost it, maybe to some woman, maybe in one of the dead cities he is always traveling through, maybe he had lost it just by looking too hard for something he knows he'll never find. But he needed to get it back, and even if searching is only a waste of time, it's a better life than just giving up.

So he gave away all of his possessions, got on his bike with just a change of clothes and a baseball bat, and rode toward the frozen north of upstate Washington. He needed to get away from people. Immerse himself in the green purity of woods. "Watch the fog," he said. "It has the only answers you'll find in San Francisco."

I've seen him move from city to city. Washington, New York, Philadelphia, L.A., San Francisco, and now Seattle. When people move close to him he always flies away, driven by some insatiable restlessness. He seems to be immune to people, can walk among them and yet not be touched. Each city is a new grid to be memorized and once the buildings are known he discards them in favor of some new and mysterious place. He does not know what he is searching for, just that it keeps him moving, and purges all his worldly possessions before they become anchors. The last thing he told me before he rode off into the dark was that he had never felt so free.

I came to the west in search of Chaos and when I arrived he left. Does this mean I'll find peace here?

I remember one bad acid trip where for an entire night I sat and painted silently while she sobbed on the couch with a bag over her head. And when I touched her she wanted to be left alone, and when I ignored her she screamed I didn't love her. And because the acid was speedy, that went on till 9 the next morning. We finally slept, even though the strychnine was shoving little metal pins into our vertebrae. And when we woke up the next evening feeling fine, clear, and sober, it was still the same thing. The craziness was beyond drugs and their clouding or exaggerating or whatever drugs do, they only refract what is actually there. There were parasites loose in us. Eating us up from the inside. Everything was falling apart and we both knew it and worked frantically at making it work, but it just wouldn't fit together, and even our friends, when we talked with them alone, would give us skeptical looks and we'd flare angry and yell at them that they didn't understand what was really going on, that love is a complicated thing, so intricate it can completely fall apart like a house of cards and we refuse to see it, go blind even in our brains, through fear of losing, hope, routine, or a force we cannot understand, a fear of darkness, a curling in warmth, to fall into sleep with company.

I come home from work exhausted. After getting high with the office crew, the lack of sleep set in. I was out only ten minutes when Alex, an ex-roommate, comes in and starts hassling his brother for money. The brother's a little computer geek who says yes too easy and Alex is quite the leech. The argument ends in Italian and Alex punches a hole in the wall before stomping out. In the apartment above, Featherhawk the coke dealer is singing old Buffalo Springfield tunes, higher up the top-floor neighbors are jamming their weird eastern vibes as we all dream in our separate beds and the city revolves around us like a great iron maiden.

Me and a girl I know went out to see the blue whale today. It had washed up dead at Fort Funston. They had a cop guarding it because local kids had carved graffiti in its side, pentagrams and the names of heavy metal bands like Motley Crue and the Scorpions. Jinny Loves Ken had been carved in the rubbery skin down below the jaw. Someone had even stolen the whale's dick. Only in San Francisco would there be someone sick enough to saw the cock off a blue whale and take it home as a souvenir. Maybe they use it as a dildo, or just put it under glass to impress their friends.

When we climbed down the sand cliffs, they were already performing the autopsy. Biologists had cut the whale up into fillets the size of pickup trucks. It had been seventy feet whole, but now the biggest piece was the tail which was only thirty feet long. The whiskers of its comb were like saw grass rising from stacks of blubber and guts. Tractors were pulling the pieces of it off in different directions. It smelled so bad that even the seagulls kept their distance, a stench big as a cloud that you could smell over a mile away and got stronger like an alarm leading you through the sand hills down the cliffs straight to the carcass, a smell so bad that it got in your clothes and hung on you the rest of the night clinging to your skin through two showers. A man with rubber gloves loaded vertebrae the size of tree stumps into the back of a pickup truck. Piles of blubber and skin were everywhere. I pressed my foot against a piece of the ribbed side and felt it give like a mattress. The oil of the body had drained into the sand and made a stain three acres wide. Tourists were taking pictures of their kids standing before huge piles of gore.

The crystal tubes of surf on the endless Pacific. Waves full of sharks waiting for all that meat to be returned to the sea. The gray sky. The sand cliffs. Silent hills covered with icehouse shrub. It had been so big cruising through its quiet blue world, the biggest thing alive continually eating the smallest. What had brought it to our shore, where we would only touch it with knives and saws, a hacking that began with the schoolchildren and continued till it didn't even resemble anything that had ever been alive? Why do humans always break things down, can only study things by tearing them apart?

Couldn't we have just given it back to the sea? Towed it out past the currents and let it sink forever into some bottomless grotto? We walked back to the car without saying a word.

I even miss your smells, the odors your body made, the way they clung to the sheets and my clothing. I miss the tastes in your mouth, even the bad ones, from stale cigarette breath to the night you chewed rose petals, the way they would change every morning to something new and strange. And I realize with sadness there were a lot of smells and tastes I could not recognize until they were gone.

Well, the guy with the hangdog look still hangs around the apartment hanging onto his girlfriend Rhonda for dear life. Shmed's wavy pompadour wisps over his forehead like a wilted rooster's comb. He always looks tired, anxious, or beaten. Guys can't stand to hang out with him because he's just too whipped. It's bad for the gender to let women treat you that low. Rhonda wants to jettison him for someone with a real income or a bigger dick or nicer car. She's the type of woman who surrounds herself with jocks just to see his veins swell. They're both too young to settle down but neither will admit it and neither can let go. She forces Shmed to eat her birth control pills and everyone kids him about how he'll grow breasts. But he's still an expert at making her cry, and their sex vibrates the walls and scares the mice back under the stove. Their lives are completely out of control as they teeter between arguments and embraces in a matter of seconds. All that matters is them, and the rest of the world is a trifling annoyance. The relationship has swollen so large there is no room for their jobs or outside lives. Friends tell them to go into therapy but it is a mess so pure they do not even try to explain it. Who cares if they can't tell if they love it or hate it? Life is out of balance so they know they're alive. I look at them and think how I was just there a few months ago. And I almost wish I was Shmed. Because in that condition of love, even though the days are a continual hell of anxiety and psychosomatic backaches, you know that you are the prime mover in someone's life. They don't do anything without thinking of you. It is a natural impulse for them to want to share things with you even if you are fighting or far away. Even if it all ends in hatred you know that for years afterwards they will think of you in their best moments, and that's a good feeling.

I walk into a nearby restaurant to get a cup of coffee. Behind the counter is a 40-year-old guy with a face like a rhinoceros's ass. His jowls flop when he walks and a reek of Vaseline steams off him. Even though he is an immense character with rough grainy skin he speaks in a high falsetto and his movements are dainty. Huge gaudy rings clasp his fingers and each hand movement as he puts cream in my coffee is accentuated by a delicate flourish. As I walk back to work holding the heat of my coffee between my hands I remember the five-alarm fire that occurred in my neighborhood this morning. An entire block of the Haight had burned down. Around 3 a.m. an arsonist had set a blaze in the skeletal construction site of a new corporate chain drugstore. The flames had eaten up the entire building complex in an inferno hundreds of feet wide. A rainfall of ash and cinders ignited the other side of the street and burned out a row of offices. As the wind changed the main flame was blown right into these structures and they were transformed into useless charcoal cubes. On the other side of the block, across the street, paint blistered and peeled off building faces, plastic signs melted from businesses. It looked like a charred Dali landscape of dripping fire escapes and misshapen plastic. The intense heat had burst all the glass panes and curtains were scorched brown in apartment windows. Supposedly, as the residents were evacuating, the sidewalk in front of their building was so hot it melted their tennis shoes and burned their feet. Now the entire block was a caved-in place of jagged wreckage and smoking wood. Tiny fires and embers smoldered here and there until the water cannon smothered them with its white beam. Minutes later some would reignite. A spiderweb of hoses and yellow police lines radiated outward from the ruin as cops barked spectators back with their bullhorns. Firemen sliced up burning hunks with chainsaws. Photographers crowded around the smoke like insects hungry for destruction. The news would add this to its steady moan of disaster and not even the neighbors down the street would bat an eye. Our eyes are naturally drawn to fire. It is an ancient attraction. The blaze turned out to have been started by two homeless men who, living like cavemen in the half-completed basement of the construction site, were tired of being woken every morning by hammers and drills. So they burned all that big noise down. Tomorrow they'll sleep in jail.

My ex-girlfriend lives in Pennsylvania. I live in San Francisco. One night I decided to propose to her and got in my car and started driving East. I got as far as Ohio before I turned back.

From the other end of the continent she is reentering my life with her letters that know exactly what to say. She is still my best friend and her phone calls sustain me for a week. I walk on my own two feet, and yet she knows just how to titillate me. I'm in love with a girl on the other side of the country. This whole situation is crazy. But it's good craziness.

Sometimes when we love someone we squeeze them so hard, attempting to push that glow we feel inside ourselves right into their skin.

When I first came to San Francisco I moved into an apartment about fifty feet from the corner of Haight and Ashbury. As soon as I heard the sounds of electric guitars and flutes trickling out the windows along the street I knew I was in a captivating place. Over the next few weeks I moved through a living blur of parties, hipsters, hippies, punks, and dreads. I met people who were lost and stoned but they weren't beaten by their world. They weren't like the dead chemical engineers I knew back East breeding poisons as they drank themselves into oblivion in the cold snows of Philadelphia. Here the city walls are painted in bright colors. The fog erases all the grime and smog. Everyone I know is a musician. There are even paintings up in the supermarkets. When I go to parties strangers are so happy to see me I wonder if I haven't really known them for years. Everyone along the side streets seems trembling on the edge of laughter. I can feel myself healing here.

I'm late for work and running out of the house in a rush. Two doors down this old woman dressed as a combination nun/nurse is sprinkling holy water from an ornate bowl all over the sidewalk and front of a neighbor's house.

Everyone on the street starts making fun of her. Three rednecks start razzing. "Look, man, voodoo! Hocus pocus! Witches!" they drawl.

"No, man, evil spirits," says some punk walking by. "That house is haunted. I used to live on Ashbury Street."

When I get to work my boss tells me there's a strict order of nun nurses that practices in the Haight. I wonder, do they live in the Anarchist Co-op?

Last Saturday night I met a Mexican guy at a party. He lives in L.A. now but is originally from Mexico City. In a room full of casually dressed yuppies he stood out in a black leather bodysuit freckled in silver studs and spikes. On his sleeve he wore an armband with a smile face in a red circle with a line drawn through it. Me and him got to talking about Mexico City. A year ago when they had the big earthquake he tried to call his family from L.A. but all the lines were down. Finally after two days of useless dialing and hair-pulling he caught a plane to Mexico.

He arrived in the city just three days after the quake. A nuclear wasteland without the fallout. Most of the buildings had been built with substandard materials so the mountains of concrete were now a flat plain of rubble. Surprisingly, if you lived on the top floor you had a better chance of surviving than if you lived on the ground floor. The stories collapsed one on top of the other, so usually the rich people who lived in the penthouses were the only ones to survive. But now the entire city looked like a giant's stomping ground.

No one escaped. On some streets the devastation was so complete that police were stationed on them to keep reporters from filming how bad it really was. In a strange and unexpected way, the quake even provided an experiment in the limits of human endurance. When a hospital collapsed, five babies were trapped in the maternity ward in the basement. It took excavators eight days to reach them. They were all still alive, after more than a week without food or water. This was an endurance record much longer than scientists previously had thought possible.

Probably what kills us quicker than anything else is our fear of dying. Being trapped underground, freaking out, going, "Oh, God! I'm gonna die! I'm gonna starve to death," uses up our energy twice as fast as normal. But the babies didn't know about fear, claustrophobia, or starvation. They probably just slept.

Before I left the East I lived in a college town and though I was well past graduation and only held there by work, I often went to parties with a high attendance of students. A new cult of drug takers evolved on the local campus. They were called Tus Heads because every Friday and Saturday night they would drink a full bottle of Robitussin DM and reduce themselves to slurred stumbling blobs. These people's conversations had a range of about two syllables, and at parties they were continually in need of babysitters. The ring leader of the group was a huge sophomore whom everyone called King Tus. He drank two bottles of Robitussin to everyone else's one. Most Sunday mornings it seemed they were picking him up out of a pool of vomit on the men's room floor. Toward the end of that year King Tus died of an overdose of barbiturates and alcohol. The group that had congealed around him kind of fell apart then. Some turned to harder drugs like cocaine and reds, others finally got laid. You know how these things go.

Late night grayness of speed come-downs, no longer wired, but twitchy and played, when sleep is a thought that just doesn't occur. All alone in the white plaster rooms of a strange new city with everyone else already crashed, in the regenerating blankness their dreams grow like Arctic flowers. Raw meat nailed to a graffitied wall. Broken images that tremble like burned veins.

Tonight I went to a neon party. Lots of leather and hair people, LSD in the wine punch. Black rubber gowns, fishnet stockings, and punks playing out their cold psychodramas. Latin boys in the living room, beatbox a smooth rap led by the DJ in the three-piece who won't leave that lesbian alone. Skinheads drag their girlfriends around the hall by their dyed hair, reenacting Og the Caveman as they rip off their flimsy black bras and shake those red nips at the crowd. Every now and then someone will ceremonially melt one of the plastic baby dolls on the mantelpiece. Around 2 a.m. everyone is drunk enough to have rediscovered Freud.

I was in the kitchen contemplating another line when in stumbles a 250-pound clone of Woody Allen. He takes one look at me and a lens falls out of his glasses. He thinks it's fallen into the trash can and immediately drops down on all fours and starts throwing trash out all over the floor, crawling around, rooting through old coffee grounds, broken eggshells, and sour milk containers. Then all these other people just standing there get down on their hands and knees and start looking through the garbage, too. The room is full of all these people crawling around on a floor covered with smelly cardboard and sticky goop. The guy finally finds his lens. It had bounced under a table and was never in the trash can at all. He holds the piece of glass over where it fell out and I watch his unsteady hand make his eye bulge and pulsate like a frog's.

Late night. Dark city streets. When I get in my car I'm so paranoid I check the back seats for dwarves. The street cleaners are coming through at six the next morning and I can't afford another ten dollar parking ticket. Everywhere I drive, street after street, there are cars, cars, cars, with less than six inches between them. It seems there are more cars than people in the city. After driving for four hours it's three in the morning and in a fifty-block area I still haven't found an empty space. Finally I am so exhausted I drive the car back to the same place I started from and park, figuring ten dollars will be a cheap price to pay for sleep.

It's 4 a.m. and I'm walking home through a London fog only it's San Francisco. Haight Street is deserted, blackened store fronts, silent lingerie, hanging palls of fog. This late night dude, one of those scungy but well-dressed men who hangs around liquor stores all night building a buzz, runs up to a car driving down the street and starts pounding on the side window going, "I got your deal. I'll make it, man, I'll make your score." God, doesn't crack ever sleep? The car just drives on.

For a minute the street is silent and the dude falls in pace behind me. We're the only two on the street so I start walking faster. Then out of the murk of the late night shadows glides this beat-up old stationwagon with no lights on. Behind the windshield it's so dark you can't see who's driving. Out of the side window issues this demonic voice hissing, "I'm the devil, hahahahaha, I'm the devil!"

The guy behind me stops and looks at the car. "So you the devil, huh?" he says.

The car turns onto a side street and starts to drive up the hill. The guy thinks for a second and takes off after it yelling, "Well, I got your deal for ya! I got your deal!" They move off into the fog until I can't hear either of them.

It's so strange to move to a new place and step into the middle of peoples' lives, a new character walking into old movies.

My friend Dada Trash was walking down the street one morning looking for a job when a bum walked up to him and said, "Hey, man, can I have a dollar so I can buy a beer?" Not 'Can I have a dollar so I can eat or help my family?' He didn't even hide it.

"Sorry, man," Dada replied, "I'm pretty broke myself."

"Well... you wanna split one?" the wino asked.

You never know if this city is trying to beat you or make you grow. It squeezes you beneath its moneys and pressures while opening up possibilities you never dreamed of. Everyone here is crazy, every day is exciting and inextricable. There is so much happening that sometimes it completely numbs you. Drive down through the low barrios, up and down hills so steep you can't believe anyone would build on them. Your car goes through chill pockets of fog, then the stifling heat of the Mission district. Drastic temperature changes occur from neighborhood to neighborhood. There is no weather here, each day is like a year of seasons. You wake up shivering, by noon you can wear shorts, evening dons long pants and jackets, night demands a winter coat. But though the air changes so drastically it is within a narrow range, it never gets hot or cold in San Francisco. Residents see snow maybe twice in their lives. Many don't own shorts. Even the rich people don't bother to build swimming pools.

Often the days are just gray flat spaces of fog. Dreary timeless afternoons. Mists that never crystallize into rain. It sounds depressing but somehow it's not. Life thrives here. People live. Walls explode with murals, bars are clogged with celebrants deliriously moving. Everyone's going and coming, fucking and loving and driving and hang gliding, scuba diving, drawing, jamming, writing, moving, shaking, dancing, painting, doing it, doing it, yeah. The optimism just doesn't go away. Even the junkies have a sense of humor. It's a place to come if you need to heal. But you won't stop once you're well, you'll keep growing and growing and we take no responsibility for what you turn into.

Chaos returned from the green woods crazier than when he left. Whatever he was looking for he obviously didn't find. But none of us ever find what we're looking for, we just kind of muddle along. Chaos has no money or place to live. He lies around all day trying to find the energy to look for a job. Six cups of coffee give him enough juice to get up and take a shit. When the sun sets he explodes into hysterics and runs about the city tearing down political flyers and ranting at strangers. He cries for no reason and has hit a raw core in his life. As we pass derelicts on the street he often comments that he will soon be one of them. At night he drives around with his hippie friends in a minivan defacing campaign ads and spraypainting real estate offices. If they meet up with a landlord they club him with baseball bats.

"If you're not part of the solution, you're part of the problem," Chaos often says, and he now admits that even pacifists must adopt the techniques of war. Violence is evil but it can be a catalyst for positive change. To sit back and do nothing is the worst thing you can do. Then you are admitting they have succeeded in making you a zero.

Chaos is no longer just a force of nature, he has become something smaller, more efficient, a shadow that slips through the night starting fires.

I lay here with a fever strangling my throat, cold and lonely in this misty city, dreaming of what lies beyond these walls in my future. Outside, headlights on Haight Street are bubbles in the hissing fog. Skinheads and hair barbarians prowl around the dark storefronts, guitar music and gurgles of party drift out second-story windows.

Basements throb with secret deals. Everyone here is wondrously asleep but our dreams shake the entire country.   Even in sleep I'm still horny and my wet dreams shoot holes in the sheets, sperm splatters against the walls, shatters through lightbulbs, cracks plaster.

Doing too much speed slowly melts the flesh, your muscles break apart in little twitching pieces, skin turns gray, fat burns away, and the skeleton slowly rises to the surface.

I'm smoking sinsemilla and broken glass. Naked legs run through my dreams and it is so dark I cannot tell if they are male or female. Last night we went to an area of the city where six blocks were closed off so all the freaks could party in the streets for Halloween. Heart of the Castro district with drag queens dancing on ledges. Two leather cops pranced around a man chained up with a rubber hood over his face, from his groin emerged a huge leather dildo which the cops snapped at with their whips. As soon as we penetrated the crowd a group of children ran by. Their leader was dressed as Satan and carried a goat's skull on a crooked wooden cross. He ran and chanted as the other children danced behind him, their faces painted like skeletons.

Carnival was everywhere as drunken ghouls stumbled about the sidewalks, crazed people banged on drums and bongos, chanting, dancing, while some dude stepped in and began playing wicked trumpet. Lots of tall women there, gender benders of every shape, size, and description, Marilyn Monroes, Brides of Frankenstein with huge synthetic breasts, the night of a thousand illusions, enough rubber titties to pave a road with, wiggling their six-foot tall derrieres, trying to pick up any gorilla, Godzilla, or loose piece of meat that moved. I saw a girl dressed as the Helga paintings and a platoon of Mickey Mouses who banged on empty water cooler jugs while singing Rolling Stones tunes. And they all raged and churned and sang their songs into the night as the cops just stood kind of sheepishly in a big circle around them, not about to fuck with anyone.

That night I dreamed I was trapped down between the buildings, feeling small and screaming. The brick walls were too big, too tall, and I ran, but in every direction were only more alleyways, crackheads, projects, she-males, rejects, all of them falling, and us caught in the flow.

My roommate tried to pacify and cheer me up with the silly stupid comments that only someone who has never been there can make. He said this break-up would be a learning experience... After a certain point in your life you don't want to learn anything new, you just want to be happy.

In an apartment upstairs a woman is screaming, "Terrible, terrible, finger!" Children moan behind laundry rippling out city windows in the wind. Concrete, brick, steel rise up in great cubes around me. I dream of worms in a poison lake, of a fetus of pure evil which swims off through dark waters to a sunken village. Of geologic amoebas that swim beneath Wisconsin. Worms made of wires that twist about my stomach of metal.

I came to the city to become a machine, a working thing with a wasted head crammed with forty hours a week of untainted boredom. Speed freaks in the leather bars, LSD cramps in my spine. A slow melting. At work I punch a computer and each day wires slither up through the keyboard and bore into my flesh, slowly replacing my nerve fibers and blood vessels. My complexion goes bad till my rubber skin gets so greasy and metallic I break out in bolts. Last night I vomited circuits and oil. I take baths in solvent and shove fuses up my ass. Broken lightbulbs are nothing to sleep on. Grease stains all over my clothing. I wake to the sound of electricity. My hand snaps off the alarm and I realize with a groan it is time to go to work again.

A Saturday night with nothing to do, no friends in the new city, and not even enough money to go get drunk in a bar. So I went down to the Tenderloin and stared at naked women for a dollar. Later as I drove through a darkened neighborhood I ogled at all the prostitutes. One tall blond had huge white breasts, little Asian girls were dressed in red and shimmering nylon, black girls in low-cut gowns. What the hell, I'll park and check 'em out. On closer inspection, they all turned out to be men.

I sit in my dark smelly room and little things feed on me. Bills that nip at the flesh like carrion birds. Slugs on the windowsill, molds in the shadowy corners, I cannot afford a bed yet and my sleeping bag is full of insects. The crawling goes all the way down to my dreams. And I can't stop them. The nightmares are getting out of control again, filled with beetle-like machines, murky demons, tears that rattle on the floor like bits of ice. At work I often cry for reasons I cannot understand. I tried to open my own store but the place is failing so bad it makes me laugh. I've never worked this hard to lose money. I sit there and watch myself sink, not able to do anything because only time will tell and stillness is agony, but so often you just have to wait, wait and hope that things get better. And there is nothing else you can do.

I have ulcers and backaches that grow from my mind. For a formless invisible force, tension sure can cause a lot of agony. Soon my stomach will be one big sore, and a doctor will replace it with a sewage treatment plant. They will stick more wires into me until I am well oiled. My fingers will be clicky sprockets, my jaw tin, with a union label for a dimple. At work they'll just roll me up to my computer, plug me in and you won't be able to tell the difference between me and the machine. Then I'll have truly adapted. The perfect city person.

Me and Dada Trash drove out to Oakland to talk to some dudes who were making t-shirts for a living. They live in a major industrial complex of cold gray pipes, dark warehouses, desolate streets of concrete. They've rented a huge studio space and turned it into rooms and print shops. Inside it's all spraypaint and psychedelic posters, t-shirts hung up to dry. Paint's splattered all over the floor, canvasses on the wall, lots of anti-Reagan propaganda, and I think yeah, people who are working the other way. The dude, a tall blond skater, just gives us a few t's to sell, he trusts us, no back East deceit. His roommate, a black guy in a shredded shirt, offers to make us stickers. Business done, we kick back and talk about beers and he shows us his zines and I tell him about mine. We talk, and it's really cool what a small world it is and I think, wow, these guys are just like us, started out as dumb teen skaters and punks, but taught themselves, and were working themselves up slowly struggling the whole damn way and scraping and clawing but making it bit by bit. And I felt really good and calm and glad for the first time in months.

Everything fizzles out and falls away. My girlfriend's letters trickle away into bigger gaps between postmen. When I call, her phone is always busy and when I finally get through she hardly listens, seems preoccupied, her life is good now, and I know I've lost her, too. I have no money at all without even the satisfaction of partying or whoring it away, just lost it all to bad luck and worse judgment in the existential universe's holy Fuck You. The relentless downward spiral continues unbroken and if you think I'm going to pieces you're right. I deserve it.

I was just in my first earthquake. Lying in my silent room reading a book when there came a sound that wasn't really a sound. It was a movement of everything in the room including myself, and you could hear it rattling through the boards and mortar, and you realize the noise/movement has grown quite loud like a silence that grows until it absorbs all sounds and there is only the movement, as you jump up and run towards the door. But before you even get out of the room it is gone like a spiritual presence, maybe there's just a little dust falling. The movement has gone back down into the earth and you realize why everyone in this city is so alive. On the street outside, shaken people begin to whoop and cheer.

The alkali purity of speed - a drug that reminds me of the Great Salt Lake desert: flat, white, and a straight line through it to drive on as fast as you want.

I remember the last time I talked to my girlfriend we had another one of those ridiculous arguments that dragged on and on over some stupid selfish little point till we got to the point where we'd stop and say, "Look, do we want this to work or not...?" but it was already over.

And she just shook her head and said, "We tried so hard to be different, but in the end we were just the same as everyone else."

One night all fucked up I wrecked my car on Market Street. I was on speed at the time and my heart just pumping away so hard that blood shot from the sliced arteries like firehoses onto the cops. Well, they pieced me back together, made me into a machine, so many bolts in my bones I clank when I walk. But if I stand on a hilltop, I can feel the lightning.

I once knew a man who was an imminent suicider and would stab himself with the first thing that came to hand. Most often that was drugs, "'Cause if you're going to kill yourself, you'd best take the funnest and longest route," he used to say.

In 1969 my father used to set the TV on the dinner table and scream at it all through the meal. My mother just sat there silently working on her ulcers, and me and my brother grew bored at Dad's repetitive rants and angry because he would never let us watch *Ultraman* instead of the news.

Last night I was at a party in Noe Valley. Nice apartment houses sloping up the steep hills. Normal people lived there. The party was thrown by a French couple who looked and acted like vampires. He had a lisp and she was anorexic. About ten of us sat in candlelight around the kitchen table drinking wine and smoking dope. A big older guy was there with this small woman and he told us of his life moving round the country. He mentioned he had been in the Tet Offensive and some of the younger people who couldn't even remember the war were quite impressed.

"Yeah," he said, "every night you were on patrol you'd walk out across these rice fields with clumps of bushes between them until you finally got to the clump of bushes that delineated your side. About fifteen feet in front of you was a clump of bushes that was their side. So you'd hunker down in between the leaves, and after awhile their bushes would start shaking and rustling and your bushes would start shaking and they'd shake and rustle back and forth at each other until finally like ghosts out of the leaves three thin men would emerge. And they'd look at you and talk back and forth a little in Vietnamese, all the while your finger sweating on the trigger wondering what they were going to do. Finally they'd look up and pull out this big long bowl, fill it with opium and start smoking. After awhile they'd offer it to you so you'd walk out of your bushes, and the four of you would squat in the clearing in between, smoking opium for about two hours till nothing functioned or thought. Then you'd both go back into your separate bushes and fall asleep till the middle of the next day. And that's how we fought Vietnam. They didn't want to fight any more than we did. We just kept being pushed against each other by these big outside forces. And when we got too close people got torn up even though that was the last thing anyone wanted to do."

"You can tell it's November," Chaos said.

"How?" I asked.

"Eyelashes," he replied as he held out his hand, between his pinched fingers were about five or six eyelashes.

"Don't ever let a witch get a hold of these," he said.

"Why?"

"Eyelashes are the frames on the windows to the soul."

There are so many images, ideas, and things that cling to the Haight. Hipsters, beats, hippies, bums, and punks walk its streets not knowing what decade it is, a timeless random search for hip, a grotesque parade of the past forty years underground. A woman sick with AIDS sits on the corner of Ashbury Street, her face streaked with sores, a woman dying of what started as a man's disease, the lowest common denominator in a place that has already seen much suffering and homelessness. She doesn't even need to ask for change, one look is enough to see her state. She is so pitiful that even those with pity turn away, try to blot her out of their consciousness because something that sad is bound to impair your daily functioning.

There are many things in the city that you just can't think about or look at. She has been cold so long that even the shivering has stopped. Past her walk bearded men with hairy legs in high heels and sheer nylons. Punks with razors collect on the corner to ritually bleed each other. Every surface is covered with a bright lichen of artwork, rock posters, and leftwing propaganda. Eight-foot drag queens walk by, shaking big hairy bosoms. Rain comes through and cleans everything, making the winos soggy as bread in water. Musicians cluster in alcoves, strumming acoustic guitars, banging African drums and empty water coolers. Things happen so fast that before you can understand them something new is happening. And you are spinning round. Moving your feet. And everyone around you is also moving. Spinning. Holding hands for a moment and letting go. To spin again. To dance. To move. Watch them dance. Even the earthquakes shake their feet and make them dance.

Daily my life degenerates into filth, masturbation, and a mindless torpor that destroys all movement. I absorb any drug that is handed to me. Crazy men on the street spot me in the crowd and adopt me as their own. At night I sit in my room staring at the wall, mindless, in spasms jerking off pools of sperm that soon fill with insects. My room grows filthier and I do not have the strength to clean it. I do not have the strength to order anything. And in a weird way I really just want it to all fall down.

Just when things couldn't possibly get worse, they did. Lenny showed up. Lenny was a scumbag. A real slime ball. One of those lowlife parasites who drifts through people's lives causing only pain, a natural channeler for bad karma. Twenty-seven years old, he had never held a steady job, dropped out of college in his sophomore year. He made ends meet as a professional sponge and male prostitute. Most often he robbed friends because they were the easiest targets and the least likely to press charges. At this juncture in his life he had moved through all his friends and was working his way through the acquaintances. An alcoholic and multi-drug abuser, Lenny often found his mind too blurred for the elaborate plans of his con games to work out. Five-foot-five with arms thin as pepperoni, he couldn't enforce his schemes through brute force and therefore often woke up bloody and beaten in strange alleyways, too hungover to remember what had gone wrong. But he kept going. Slime is like that, it just keeps sliding through things.

Lenny was an acquaintance of one of my roommates. Fate brought him to our door the one night we left it unlocked. He just walked on in, made himself a nice big meal from the refrigerator, and helped himself to our wine. By the time Andy got home from the Kennel Club, Lenny had polished off two bottles of red and sat on our couch with a big yellow-toothed grin. Andy blew up at him. "Out, scum! I don't want you in this house! Last time we kicked you out we told you not to come back! I can't believe your fucking nerve! What the... Wha... Shit! That's my fucking wine! Out! Now!"

"Bruno said I could stay," Lenny replied with a sheepish grin.

Bruno was back East for two weeks. Lenny said he had stayed with him in New York and Bruno said he could crash here for a night or two. Bruno's name was on the lease. And there was no way to contact him to find out if Lenny was lying. He hadn't left a phone number.

"Okay, okay," said Andy, "you can crash here for about four hours, but by the time I get up tomorrow morning I want you out."

"Okay," said Lenny. "You want some wine?"

"My own fucking wi—! You bastard, four hours, no more."

Andy was pretty drunk so he went into his bedroom and passed out. When I got up and went to work Lenny was still there, halfway through his third bottle of wine, eyelids drooping, and each word just a blur. I thought he was a friend of one of the roommates and therefore didn't ask him to justify his presence. As soon as I left he went into my room and rifled through my drawers and pockets until he found the $800 I had stashed in my vest. Then he left, too.

That afternoon Andy was woken up by a call from Bruno.

"Andy, have you seen Lenny?"

"Yeah, he crashed here last night. Look, Bruno, I don't like that scumball hanging around here."

"Shit, he's already been there. Jesus, Andy, he was back here in New York a couple days ago. He stole $600 from me. That's how he showed up in San Francisco again."

"Fuck, what's he doing? Traveling around the country robbing everyone he knows?"

"Kinda looks like it."

Andy hung up the phone and ran into the living room to beat the shit out of Lenny. But he was already gone.

When I got home I immediately noticed the money was gone,

too. It was all the money I had in the world and I needed to pay rent that week.

Of course, we called the cops. They sent a man over who basically said they could do nothing. Nobody had actually seen Lenny take the money. True, he was the only stranger in the house when it had been stolen but that was only circumstantial evidence. The officer was willing to fill out a report but he couldn't arrest Lenny and the police didn't usually bother to investigate cases that involved such a small sum of money. I have no faith in the police. They are either useless or destructive. They're willing to kick down your door and beat up your friends when you're having a party, or fine you a thousand dollars and put you on probation for a year for smoking a joint in the park, but when it comes to being robbed in your own house they can't do a damn thing.

Me and the roommates began to put out feelers, threading the phone lines with our calls, tracking down Lenny's friends. He didn't have many left. So we began to track down his acquaintances. There were a lot of them. He got around. And everywhere he had gone he took more than he left. A career leech. A dealer in bad vibes. Someone I didn't even know had inexorably fucked up my life. I had hardly even seen him. All we had done was given him a place to sleep and our wine, and he had taken everything I had. The money was earmarked for the rent on my room. I would lose my home to this parasite who drifted through my life for less than eight hours.

This was the worst thing that could have happened at the worst time. We kept calling his acquaintances, most of whom were willing to help us kill him if we could find him. Unfortunately, most of them had given up on revenge and filed him as a loss. But I wasn't ready to take it lying down. I wasn't going to just let it happen to me without at least trying to do something about it. We finally got ahold of a speed dealer who had seen him the night before. He thought Lenny was staying in a flophouse down in the Tenderloin.

The Tenderloin, a synonym for Hell. Grimy buildings festering in the mist with a smell of piss and vomit. Shadowy figures shuffle along its cracked pavements like creatures in a dream. One stretch of sidewalk is covered with the homeless and near dead. Ragged tents are pitched in front of condemned buildings. People with scabbed faces live in shopping carts, eat from garbage cans. A man on the corner looks like he hasn't washed in three years. The only way to tell the dead from the merely drunk is to wait for the inanimate ones to stink of rotting flesh. Sandwiched between the abandoned tenements are cheap flophouse hotels, porno stores, peep shows and lowlife dives, bars where mummified alcoholics sit on lonely stools and mumble to themselves. After dark, screeching crack dealers parade the sidewalks, threatening to hit those who will not buy. Prostitutes and down-and-out she-males swish about in search of stray cocks and diseases, the money is just an excuse.

We found Lenny's hotel on Turk Street. A mission for the homeless. Nothing like giving scum charity. When we got out of the car there were lines of piss every five feet along the sidewalk. We stepped over a drunk and rang the bell on the iron gate. The manager was a fat old guy with a red beard you could see through. You could tell he was suspicious of everyone because almost all of his tenants had done something wrong. He told us that Lenny wasn't there but wouldn't let us in the iron gate to check and see if he was lying. We told him what the deal was, explained how Lenny had stolen a lot of money from us and some people in New York, how he was a slime who oozed from place to place stealing things, causing trouble. We offered to pay the manager thirty bucks if he'd tell us when Lenny came back. As soon as we made the offer I knew he'd never call us. Even though we were where Lenny was staying I could feel him moving further away, slipping between our fingers, into out there.

Lenny wasn't there so we had to go look for him. We had checked through all his ex-friends and acquaintances, that meant he must be out working. So we began to check the street corners, talking the whole time about how we were going to rend his flesh useless, where the blows would land, how the groin would bruise. My friend Dada Trash had a skull-shaped ring and he discussed with relish how it could be used to gouge out an eye. Then he stopped for a moment and something invisible but cold spread across his face. "Wait a second," he said, "this guy's a street hustler. We gotta make sure we don't draw any blood. Really, his blood could be as dangerous as venom."

So we walked those ugly streets searching for a face we barely knew, a countenance that I had seen for a vague instant the night before, a single flash in a city of faces. We passed all the fifteen-year-old boys smiling at the tourist businessmen driving by in their sedans. We went into every scumball bar, smoky neon-lit places full of drug-dealing weasels, emaciated loners, places without smiles, where everything was eaten by melancholy. Rooms full of the forlorn, where every edge was blurred by alcohol or some more exotic poison. Lost faces full of hard luck stories and dreams that had died so long ago they were completely forgotten. Not even the old Motown tunes on the jukebox could revive them. Murmuring loveless lives. Drunks. Junkies. But no Lenny. In all the ugly faces, he was still faceless. And something grew in us as we kept looking. Something huge and beast-like, a nameless thing.

By the end of the night I didn't care if we got our money back. I just wanted to hit him. To feel his soft flesh hurting in my hands. To know that I was forcing back into his life the agony he had put into mine. I was chasing the leech and the city had swallowed us both. I didn't mind losing the money that much, but I was beginning to lose faith in my fellow man. What kind of a world could produce a place like this? I was walking among the dead and could feel them draining the life from me. For a moment the thought flashed across my mind that this was all a conspiracy, that this much couldn't go wrong in my life without some insidious plot being behind it all. But then I laughed out loud at how ridiculous the idea was. Who would waste their time? For the rest of the night we walked lower and lower into the gloom of the buildings but we never found who we were looking for.

Around 3 a.m. we went back to Lenny's flophouse but the manager had already kicked him out. And then we knew we had really lost him. He would just drift on to another city to cause more pain, unscathed. He would probably live out his life without ever having to pay for his actions, escaping the wrath of all his victims, leaving them without even a target. I was so angry I wanted to punch a wall, but I would just hurt myself. My anger could only go back into Lenny, it had to be pounded into his flesh. But I would never see him again. And that anger would never really leave me.

I was the jinx. My bad luck spilled over my edges and landed on everyone around me. I went to work for another company, profits plummeted, people developed viruses, called in sick, had accidents on the freeway. This shit went on till they fired me. The next job always paid less. The people there more sullen, poorer, down. They slipped on wet floors, broke ankles, fell off scaffolds, moaned they had no health insurance. The guys at the warehouse called me "el hombre malo." I didn't want to hurt poor people so I quit, but I had to feed myself. The mailman cracked his skull on my front step delivering my welfare check and food stamps. My apartment house burned down, killing everyone but me. God, the sound of those families screaming.

I ran from the inferno thinking enough is enough and tried to catch a cab out of the city into the country where there weren't enough circumstances for things to go wrong. Unfortunately, the cab ran into a traffic light at an intersection and a bus trying to swerve around us rolled over and burst into flames, thirty passengers on board, shishkebab arms and scrambled egg brains. In a panic I lifted a manhole cover and crawled off into the sewers hoping that there was finally a place where I wouldn't spur disaster. But I'd made my biggest mistake. I'd gone underground. Close to the fault line. The turds in the water around me began to tremble as I realized the earthquake was coming.

What did I come in search of? Lost dreamers in a vaguer dream? Poverty, struggle, and an endless grinding of my raw backbone against a concrete wall? Blind junkies already dressed for the dead, so sunk in their chemicals that not even the shrieking guitars can claw the moss from their eyes? I didn't come here for robbery and mind rape. The buildings get taller and taller and there is no one in them. But they don't grow. I get lower. Sink into the underground. I get down.

Energy builds up in city walls, people in tiny rooms with no windows to blow off pressure, their auras clashing, rubbing against each other in these tiny white cubes beginning to throb, little stages where we act out our psychodramas, glow karma, spit word games, lie, cheat, steal, eat. Little rooms hold all the energies in buildings till the city lights up the locale for miles around. We laugh, we frown. And eventually learn to live together.

I've lost faith in maybes, and hopefullys too for that matter. Now I always think about what could be or what might be, but never what will be, because what should be, isn't, and therefore, won't.

Speed downs. Violent two day withdrawals from a drug that locks into your cardiovascular system like the highest gear of an engine. You must keep doing speed until you stop and the crash is as low as the high. On the drug you can get so much done, do incredible things, double your productivity, work hours on end all night because sleep is such a ridiculous thing, a thought that never occurs. Wrenching sexual spasms assault you like automobile accidents, forcing you to feel the muscles of your soft parts. But afterwards you pay with two days of twitching exhaustion, a thoughtless empty head, diarrhea, no attention span, and a nameless ceaseless depression. Speed gives you half of next week today. But it doesn't give you anything more - it just allows you to have everything now.

Chaos was ranting. "Safety standards in Russia are almost nonexistent. In some areas where they have chemical companies it's gotten so bad, the mandatory retirement age is 45. There's some lake in the Ukraine that's so contaminated, when they throw dead cats in it, the bodies just dissolve."

She wouldn't take an answer for an answer, kept reading into it, asking questions, giving answers nowhere near the truth, or any possible truth I could have thought of, looking, probing for things, coming to conclusions out of the blue, everything I said, till I just wanted to shut up, sit there and say nothing, but that just let her go on uninterrupted, making up some kind of false world tooled to the sharp angle of her anger. I couldn't stay silent, had to yell that No, that's not it! That's not it at all, it's just words! Just words! Misunderstandings. Sounds that instantly go away. Why do we let words do this to us? Put us in such pain, it's like poking in our diarrhea for signs of religion. Words are just pieces of things and everybody sees the pieces differently, so we'll never put them together the same, we will always argue. "Please, don't say anything. Just hold me."

She stopped with a scowl. Looked at me for a second. And then kept on bitching.

FOUR

My wallet got stolen on Christmas Eve. There's nothing like a pickpocket who works the holidays. My luck seemed to have a limitless ability to go down, from gray to black. Christmas really is the darkest day of the year. My ex-girlfriend had been slowly weeding her way back into my life. It started with postcards. Just a few at first, precious little squares that told me it wasn't over, that there was still hope. True, we had failed once, but we could work it out, try again, learn from our mistakes and make something good, we could make a second go. She lived on the East Coast, I was on the West, we could meet somewhere in between. The postcards became long letters, tortured cries of loneliness and fear, of learning to be single and alone, after being two for so long - the same things I was going through. So, of course, I leapt at every word, embraced their unspoken maybes, built sandcastles in my mind. We talked over the phone, long sobbing conversations, and other times it seemed no one else could make us laugh so much. It was so easy to talk to each other, our new lovers were bores, thought only of their own needs, lacked tenderness, interest, or a sense of humor.

That last year together had been horrible but we repainted it in our minds, added gaudy bright colors that just hadn't been there, tried to make that wretched apartment full of roaches and peeling paint into some kind of lovers' paradise - but it was all just lies we were telling ourselves and each other. Yet at this time in our lives we were ready to believe lies. We would swallow anything. Our phone bills were over a hundred dollars a month - almost as much as the rent we had paid to live together. But this was a bodiless torture, two voices desperate in the void of operators, two physical fuck junkies, sex addicts, subsisting on a diet of mere words. But the touches of our new lovers left us speechless. They were strangers. We wanted to know that body in our bed. We needed to feel there was really someone behind those lips. So we reached back for a desperate snatch of the past we never had. Long distance we built a glass castle inhabited by two people who weren't really there. Frightened people, newly alone, a continent apart. No wonder our friends told us to just start over. To put it behind us. But things don't end that easy.

The day after Christmas, she flew me back to see her. I spent Christmas Eve and day alone, far from my family, in an unheated apartment cocooned in a freakish San Francisco cold spell. It snowed in the city for the third time in twenty-five years. With my luck I think I could have seen snow at the equator. The temperature inside and out was thirty-one degrees. I could see my breath in my bedroom. The flu hit me as I went to catch my plane. Fever made the whole airport woozy. As soon as we took off the sibilant sound of the engines lulled me to sleep. I awoke over the colored spiderwebs of the East, shopping malls and suburbs emitted nebular auras like patterns at the ending of Kubrick's 2001, even Newark, New Jersey looked beautiful in the cold night air.

She was waiting for me at the baggage claim, her hair grown out in a style she would never wear for me when we lived together. We couldn't stop kissing. She didn't care that I was sick. That night and the next day all we did was fuck. As one of us drifted to from sleep we would find the other's hands on us, caressing to a friction that after the climax had burned us out so completely we would fall back into sleep. It was like that all day, a continual bobbing between passion and oblivion. But it was already flawed. I could feel the old tension creeping in like a twinge in my back, a watching of every word I said, spasms of anger or sadness that came out of nowhere, the suspicion that this couldn't last. She felt it too but neither of us said anything for a few hours. That night we watched a movie in silence. In bed, right before sleep, she rejected my touches saying she was tired. The next morning it was there, raw and suppurating. This wasn't working. It couldn't. We had a calm and pleasant conversation in which we came to the conclusion that we weren't going to live together again - ever. Oh, the love and sex were there, but our lives just wouldn't fit together. Right people, wrong goals. Square pegs, round holes.

We would try and make it a good week anyway. Avoid this grim conclusion with constant sex and stimulants. We could still just enjoy each other's company. But there was too much water under the bridge. After the marriage, you can't go back to dating. An argument lurked behind every sentence, every simple throwaway remark that hurt the other's feelings in a complicated way. Out of the silence one of us would suddenly get furious or just as easily cry. After the morning conversation I could feel her moving away, could see her asking herself, "Well, what's the point, now that it'll never become anything real?" Whenever I touched her she was ice. I was sick, world beaten, I needed some warmth. That afternoon we drove up to see a summer camp she had worked at.

It was in upstate New York. Gray skies, denuded trees, icicles drooling like long tongues from the granite beside the road. We unhooked the chain between two rock posts and drove into the state park. The road was rutted and covered with dead leaves and fallen branches. We passed two frozen lakes, their polar surfaces circulatory systems of inch-thick cracks. Beneath them cold fish dull in a slow motion world. The mountains were too big for any picture, their beauty saurian, mystic, older than the Indians who may have understood them. When we got to the camp she squatted in the underbrush to pee. The sight of her drove me wild. It was the first time I had ever seen a woman relieve herself in the woods and there was something feral, bestial about it, raw sexuality, birth on dead leaves, the Earth Mother that lives in us all.

"Woman in the wild," I said.

"You make it sound like a cheap porno novel," she replied petulantly.

A male and a female deer nibbled gray grass on a ridge nearby. As we walked closer to them they ran away. Perhaps they could feel it in us. The camp was typical: outhouses, mess hall, swimming dock, flagpole. But the land was beautiful. Huge granite boulders, jagged ravines, tall trees, wildlife. I could easily understand why she had come here all those years. I wondered how it looked in the summer when everything was green and alive, I could picture her working with the disabled and emotionally disturbed children, the camp nurse dispensing bandaids, calamine lotion, and mother love. Where did I fit into all this? Then I realized, I didn't.

We hiked up a dirt road to see a battered little graveyard from the 1800s. It lay inside a collapsed stone wall, headstones almost worn smooth, tangled briars and green moss erasing the icons of these hill people's lives. Over the summer she had performed a ritual there with a dead crow and a human skull. She and another counselor from the camp had spoken in tongues, babbled incantations beneath the moon, the skull and bird were buried at opposite ends of the collapsed ring of stones, they asked the advice of the spirits buried there. The tombstones said nothing. The ritual was meant to chase away evil spirits. Maybe she had just chased them into my life. We left the graveyard and fought our way through a field of briars, thistles, and vines. She showed me the ruined foundation of a colonial house. More lives that had wandered off and gone wrong. When we got back to the car she said she was going to move back here.

I would have lasted about two weeks in the place. Sure, it was beautiful and regenerating, but I needed my big city poisons. On the way home in the car we began to argue. As usual these arguments were trite and ridiculous, excuses to destroy things. By the time we got back to her apartment we were exchanging soft spoken intimacies that made each other cry. Truths more painful than angry lies. It wasn't a fight anymore, it was just very, very sad. For an hour we lay on her couch holding each other and crying hysterically. Then she took me to the train station and bought me a ticket for Philadelphia. On the platform, it was snowing and we held each other sitting on a bench. Both of us were weeping, not caring if anyone saw us.

"I'm sorry, I've really let you down," she said.

I lied and said, "No, you haven't."

The train slid from the night, a bright-eyed serpent ready to take me from all hope of paradise. From my window I watched her body shrink away into the snow until I was left staring at only my own reflection in the dark pane.

After we broke up for the last time, I went to my parents' house and washed her smells out of my clothing.

There was nothing more to say. We both just cried a lot. I got on the train and went to Philadelphia where I drank all night in a down-and-out blues bar with a band of cats blowing sad jazz, me and a couple of old friends were the only white people there and strangers were buying me drinks because they all could tell I was broke in little pieces. In three days I slept on separate floors in four different states although one of them was just a passing out in New Jersey. I had a case of the flu at the time so I figured it was best to take as many drugs as possible, like alcohol, speed, blow, weed, and magic mushrooms, but I must admit that the shrooms were just something slipped to me in a container of spaghetti I munched in Pennsylvania, or was it Delaware, I'm not sure where, but there was this big splat of diarrhea on a wall there and this guy and his girlfriend were getting their pictures taken in front of it.

The East Coast smelled dirtier than I had remembered it, but in South Philly that stench was a flag of nostalgia. Dirtier. More poisoned. More dead cars in junkyards, lakes of shit, broken hypos on the beaches. And it kept saying, "Go back west. Go back west." Like a murmur below the pollution, a shadow under the edge of cities, in those strange barrels you see in empty fields, but never brave enough to peel the lid off, to look into that obliterating chemical darkness...

A dinosaur eats a small duck on the cover of *National Geographic*. It's late at night and I sit in a thin light wiring threads of ink on paper, but there is something wrong, and the words creep to the edge of the page and leap off suicidal into the darkness... Baby, don't take it light but I make my mojo in the darkness. She was light, I dark. I light. I dark. Light. Dark. Gray.

When I got back from the East, I sat in my room and did nothing but drugs for an entire day. A continual hand to orifice ritual of bongs, bottles, and straws, I consumed my entire narcotics collection: acid, speed, coke, weed, Quaaludes, and lots of tequila sucked down in an attempt to blur the edges, to make everything turn soft and go away. But it all just stayed there glaring, stinging, mocking, saws on raw nerves. I still felt cold sober no matter what I put into me until around 3 a.m. when my depression cut through the speed and I reached the smooth oblivion of sleep. The next day when I went to work they fired me. They didn't give much of a reason. I guess it was all in my face.

She was a nurse. Working every day in a cancer ward cleaning the shit pans of rotting flesh, minds benumbed, another pawn in a healthcare system going bankrupt to keep terminal grannies alive an extra two weeks. No Codes they called them. Do not resuscitate in case of seizure. On machines that cost five thousand a day while people a quarter of their age grow scars because they couldn't afford stitches. They'll bankrupt Medicare in ten years. "People live too long," she told me.

True. We get tired. Sometimes long before our time, so we speed things up with razors, wrists, lines, speed, it's all the same thing. It all goes in the same general direction. Towards the edge. She was tired, too. Burned out from feeling for people, from trying not to feel. Young people came through the ward. Kids sometimes. Now a mother was there, just forty with two almost teenage boys. And she just tried so hard not to feel. Even turned off her friends, wouldn't touch anything. But when that mother goes she doesn't know if she can keep working. So too she turned away from me.

Maybe it is because I am broken, but dreams and reality flow freely together now and I no longer have the strength or desire to hold them apart. I pursue my dreams because I have nothing left in my heart to follow. Maybe our dreams for the future are little more than reflections of our past. When it was all over and everything was said and done, I realized these problems of love had left me so wasted and confused I couldn't tell today's flashbacks from yesterday's premonitions.

Jon Longhi lives in San Francisco where he sells comic books, smut, and underground literature for a living. He has read his work at literary festivals including LitEruption in Portland, Oregon, rock concerts including the 1992 & 1994 Lollapalooza Festivals, public libraries, college campuses, bookstores, cafes, and bars. This is his third book.